D1736323

Meet me in the Penalty Box

USA TODAY BESTSELLING AUTHOR

CALI MELLE

Playlist

Dancing with a Stranger - Sam Smith, Normani

Feel - Post Malone, Kehlani

Ride for Me - Daniel Di Angelo

Strawberry Skies - Kid Travis

Long Nights - 6LACK

Muse - Bayou

HER - Chase Atlantic

Control - Pablo, Preston Pablo

Die For You - The Weeknd

Snow on the Beach - Taylor Swift

3AM - Russ, Ty Dolla $ign

This one is for the ones looking for that love that sets your soul on fire.

Prologue

Nico

As I walked off the ice and headed back to the locker room, my hair was soaked and stuck to the back of my neck. There was nothing like hitting the ice for practice and having your coach tell you that you're not practicing with pucks. After the loss that we had on Sunday, I wasn't surprised. We got spanked and it wasn't the pleasurable kind of spanking.

"Damn, that man is ruthless," Lincoln mumbled as we both dropped down onto the bench beside each other. He was in his rookie year too, so we were both working our asses off to prove that we belonged playing on this level.

Ice hockey was competitive as hell and if you weren't keeping up with the best, you'd easily get left behind. Dropping back to the AHL wouldn't be a death sentence, but it wasn't what I wanted. I wanted it all, or nothing.

And luckily, I was right where I needed to be in

terms of impressing our coach and being an asset to the team.

Coach Anderson didn't fuck around and I wasn't about to be the one who got on his bad side. We had one issue this entire season and it was about me getting into some unnecessary fights. I dialed it back a bit since we had a talk about it and everything had been good between us ever since.

"Cirone," Miles, one of our new equipment guys, said as he walked over to me. "Let me get your practice socks so I can get you new ones."

I pulled the clear tape from the material and balled it up and set it on the bench beside me before I continued undressing. Miles looked at the ball of tape and held out his hand for it as I handed him my socks.

"Do you want me to throw the tape out for you?"

My eyes widened and I shook my head. "Absolutely not."

Wes chuckled from a few guys down. "You never touch Nico's tape," he warned Miles. Wes and I played on the same team together in the AHL before we were moved up to the NHL. He knew my weird quirks and superstitions.

"What's the deal with the tape?" Miles questioned the two of us, genuinely interested.

I shrugged off the rest of my equipment and put it all back in its respective place. "My mom started this thing when I was a kid. I used to piss her off with leaving balls of tape everywhere, so every season she would collect them. It kind of started this weird thing that I do now."

Wes laughed again and Lincoln shook his head. "Go on, tell him more," Lincoln urged. "It gets even more interesting."

I looked between my two teammates. "Like neither of you have your own weird things you do." I paused and directed my attention at Wes. "You sleep in your damn suit every night before a game."

Wes simply shrugged. "It's good luck, bro."

"And so is my ball of tape."

Miles looked between the three of us. "You know what, I don't need to know the specifics. I know now to leave your tape untouched, so we're good."

He quickly moved away from all of us and everyone went back to their routine. Some of the guys headed into the shower to wash away the sweat before leaving. Wes walked over to me as I grabbed my keys, phone, and wallet.

"What are you doing tonight, Nico? Some of us are going to meet up at that new club Mirage. You game?"

I shrugged, even though my body was telling me I needed to go home and go to bed. "Sure, why not. I'm going to run home and shower and I'll meet you guys there?"

"Sounds good," Wes said with a smile before he left the locker room. I wasn't far behind him and some of the other guys came out in a larger group. I was still getting to know a lot of the guys and they had been pretty accepting so far.

After hopping into my black Mercedes, I headed out through the ramp that led down to where all the players parked. The man sitting at the booth lifted the gate and waved as I drove through. My apartment was only a five-minute drive from the arena and there wasn't much traffic so I got home without any issues.

From one parking garage to another, I slid my car into its spot and took the elevator up to my floor. It was a building of condos and each floor was its own separate unit. I didn't make enough of a salary for a place like this, but my mother had an insane trust built for me and she left me a fortune when she passed away.

The thought weighed heavily on my heart and as I stepped into the shower, I couldn't help but tilt my head back and wonder where she was in the universe. I hoped wherever she was, I was making her proud. She was diagnosed with cancer when I was finishing up college. Her prognosis wasn't good and she didn't last very long with us after she found out.

She was alive when I was drafted into the NHL and I'd never forget the look on her face. It was a memory I had cemented inside my brain. She never got to see my NHL debut, but I knew she was with me that day. I missed her, but there was nothing I could do about it now except hope that I was continuing to make her proud.

After showering, I got dressed and added my ball of tape to the massive one I'd been collecting during the season. I had been keeping it in my guest room and thankfully, no one ever asked to see inside the room. To the guys, it wasn't anything to be ashamed of. Someone who didn't understand it might not find it as amusing.

By the time I left my apartment, it was already well into the night and I was pulling into the parking lot at the club by ten-thirty. Wes had already texted me to let me know they were here and to head to the VIP section.

"Took you long enough," Lincoln said as I took a seat next to him in the booth. There was a bottle of champagne in a bucket in the center of the table, but everyone had mixed drinks and was taking shots.

I shrugged as I grabbed one of the shots and swallowed it back. The liquor burned as it slid down my esophagus, but I welcomed the feeling. "Let's be real— you guys were probably here for five minutes before I showed up."

Wes clapped his hand on my shoulder and gave me a swift shake. "Hey, buddy," he said with a smile in his voice. "Linc was just missing you, is all."

Lincoln laughed loudly. "I'm here for one thing and one thing only tonight," he said with a smirk. "And you are not it, Cirone."

"Bummer," I chuckled as I grabbed one of the mixed drinks that Wes had. Otto, Mac, and Cole were sitting in the booth talking to some girls who had wandered over. A few of the other guys were here somewhere, but who knew where they wandered off to.

Lincoln stood up from where he was sitting. "I'm heading out to scope out the scene. Either of you want to come with me?"

Wes shook his head as he leaned back in his spot and slowly sipped his bourbon and ginger ale while pulling out his phone. "Nah. I'm just going to lay low for a little."

Lincoln glanced over at me. "Cirone?"

I shrugged as I picked up my drink and stood up. It

was the same thing Wes was drinking. "Fuck it. I don't have anything else going on, so I'm down."

Lincoln smiled and he began to wander through the VIP section. I followed after him as the sound of the bass pounded through the speakers and directly into my bones. It was loud as hell but the DJ had a nasty mix going, so I was feeling it as we walked down the stairs and into the main area of the club.

I waded through the sea of dancing bodies and lost Lincoln somewhere along the way. I didn't need him as my wingman. I was highly capable of finding someone without him. Plus, Wes was a better wingman than he was anyway.

As I pushed my way through the throng of people, eventually the crowd broke open to where the bar was. My eyes scanned the area and I took a seat as I finished my drink. Setting it down, I ordered another when the bartender came over to me. Just as I placed my order, someone ran into my back, pushing me forward slightly in my seat.

"Oh my god, I am so sorry."

The sound of her voice slid across my eardrums like silk and I slowly turned around to face her. She was still standing close and I caught a whiff of her floral perfume. The corners of my lips lifted as her blue eyes met mine. Under the flashing colored lights from above, her blonde hair changed hues with each flash.

She was petite and looked like I could probably bench-press her entire body. A tight black dress hugged her curves and I allowed myself the opportunity to quickly check her out as she moved to the seat next to me.

"There are so many damn people in here. Someone pushed me into your back." She paused for a moment, pulling a credit card from her clutch. "Let me buy you an apology drink?"

Reaching out, I placed my hand over hers and pushed the card back into her small bag as I shook my head. "You don't owe me anything." I smiled at her as she turned to face me. "I have a better idea. How about I buy you a drink instead?"

My eyes were drawn to her plump lips. They were stained a dark red from her lipstick and I wanted the matching stains on my own lips. "I like that idea."

"What are you drinking?"

Just as I asked her, the bartender walked back over with my drink and I listened as she ordered a vodka soda. I assessed her as she was talking to the bartender. My eyes traveled over her high cheekbones and down her straight nose. She reached up and tucked her straight hair behind her ear.

She turned to face me. "Do they make their drinks strong here?"

I glanced at the bartender and took a sip of my own drink. "Usually. Judging by this drink, I think it's safe to say they do. Is this your first time here?"

She nodded. "I just moved here a week ago for a new job. One of the girls I met through work invited me out here, but she brought her boyfriend and I'm not in the mood to be a third wheel."

Luckily for her, I was only looking for a second wheel.

"What do you do for work?" I inquired as she got her drink and took a sip of it.

She set her glass down just as the DJ switched the song to a different one. "I'm a photographer." Her face lit up and she began to move in her seat to the beat of the music. "Why is that always a question people ask when you first meet someone?"

"I feel like it's an easy icebreaker," I said with a shrug. "Plus, you did say that you just moved here because of your new job, so I figured I'd be polite and ask about it."

This earned a smirk from her. "Ah. Trying to make it seem like your intentions are pure and wholesome, right?"

I laughed and shook my head at her. "My intentions are only the purest and most wholesome." I leaned closer to her, my lips brushing against her ear. "I'm actually an angel and as innocent as they come."

She snorted and pushed me back before hopping out of her seat. "I highly doubt that," she winked as she grabbed her drink with one hand and grabbed my bicep with the other. "Dance with me?"

I grabbed my drink and slowly rose to my feet. "I thought you'd never ask."

Her palm was warm against mine as I threaded my fingers through hers and followed her into the crowd. She abruptly stopped and I dropped her hand, grabbing her waist to hold her upright as I crashed into her back.

She lifted her arm up, snaking it around the back of my neck as she began to move in front of me.

Her back was pressed flush against my torso. We had about a foot difference in height so her ass was just below my pelvis as she began to roll her hips. I moved along with her, grinding against her as I slid my hand across the front of her dress, stopping with my fingers splayed across the bottom of her stomach.

Holding her drink in one hand, she spun around in my grip and I was holding the small of her back as she faced me. Her other arm was back around my neck and her velvet skin slid against mine. I wanted to toss my glass onto the floor so I could hold her with both hands. I wanted to explore her body and get lost in the valleys and planes of her torso.

We were pressed flush against each other, two strangers in the darkness of the club as we moved together to the music. She leaned her head back, her ocean blue eyes colliding with mine as she gazed up at me. Her lips parted slightly and my gaze dropped down to her mouth before finding her eyes again.

"Kiss me," she murmured. I could barely hear her over the music, but her body spoke louder. "Make me forget it all."

My face dipped down to hers. "What are you trying to forget, love?"

"The asshole who broke my heart."

I pulled back slightly, a ghost of a smile playing on my lips as I searched her eyes. "So, you're looking for someone to replace the memory of him tonight?"

She flashed me her bright white teeth and her eyes danced under the flashing lights. "Exactly."

Everyone around us continued to dance along to the music, but we weren't moving with them anymore. Instead, my face was dipping down to hers and I was claiming her mouth with my own. She tasted like the vodka she was drinking and her nails dug into the back of my neck as I traced the seam of her lips with my tongue.

Gripping onto her waist, I slid my tongue against hers, breathing her in as she moved against me. This wasn't usually my style with a girl that I had just met. I mean, by the end of the night, I was usually on my way back to their place with them, but I usually tried to play it cool at first.

She made it clear what her intentions were and I wasn't going to deny her a fucking thing.

Our tongues were tangled together and there was an urgency behind our kiss. My lips bruised hers and I wanted more. Fuck playing it cool, fuck waiting till later. Abruptly breaking apart, I left her breathless and she stared up at me with wide eyes.

I pulled at the material of her dress as I spun on my heel. Her hand slid into mine and I headed through the crowd. I needed to get her alone. Somewhere I could do whatever she wanted me to do.

She followed along after me as we moved toward the back of the building and discarded our drinks along the way. We climbed the stairs and I led her through the VIP area. I caught Wes's eye as I strode past the booth the guys were in. He raised an eyebrow and nodded in approval. There was a back room tucked off to the side. I had no idea what was in it, but we were about to find out.

Grabbing the handle, I turned it to the side and it opened with ease. I pushed it open and pulled the girl in with me before shutting it behind us. Her hands were on my back and heat rolled off her in waves.

"I can't see a thing. Is there a light in here?"

I turned around to face her, my fingers trailing up her neck and across her jaw. "I don't want anyone to interrupt us."

I could hear the smile in her voice in the darkness. "Good idea."

She leaned up on her toes and our mouths collided in a rush. Her arms were around the back of my neck and she ran her fingers through my hair as she held on to me. I grabbed her hips and slowly backed her up until she was flush against something.

"Wait," she broke away, breathless. "I don't even know your name…"

I pulled away for a moment, sliding my hand into my pocket as I pulled out my phone to check our surroundings. It was just a storage closet and there was a worktable behind her. Turning off the screen, I slid it back into my pocket before I grabbed her thighs and lifted her up.

The sharp intake of her breath filled the room and her hands clutched at my shoulders as I had her sitting on the table with me standing between her legs. My cock throbbed in my pants and she hooked her legs around my waist, pulling me flush against her.

"Nico," I told her as I dropped my mouth to her neck. "But you can call me whatever the fuck you want."

"Mmm, Nico," she hummed as she reached for the bottom of my dress shirt and pulled it out of my pants. Her nails were sharp against the skin on my back. "Different. I like it."

"I like the way my name sounds rolling off your tongue, but you know what I really want to hear, love?"

She looked up at me as I pulled the straps of her dress down her arms. "What's that?"

"I want to hear you screaming it instead."

I slid the straps of her dress down to her elbows before trailing my hands across her collarbones. My lips found hers again as my fingers traced the dips and curves of her body. Sliding the material under her breasts, the feel of her skin was soft against my palms and I rolled her nipples between my fingers.

She moaned into my mouth and I swallowed the sound. Her hands found the waistband of my pants and she worked them open. Shifting my hips back, I gave her access to my cock as she slid her hands under my boxers.

A pounding sounded on the other side of the door and she stilled against me with my cock throbbing in her hand. "Someone knows we're in here," she breathed against my lips.

"Fuck," I mumbled as I released her breasts and pulled back. Whoever was on the other side knocked on it again and I heard my name. "Goddammit." I grabbed the straps of her dress and pulled them back up to cover her up. "Hold on."

Her heels hit the floor as she dropped down off the table and I pulled up my zipper and buttoned my pants as I walked over to the door. The hinges groaned as I pulled on it with force, feeling the frustration building inside. My balls ached and I needed to be inside her.

Wes was standing on the other side with a look of regret on his face. "Sorry to interrupt, bro, but I need your help with Linc."

"What about him? I'm not his babysitter."

He frowned and swayed a bit. "He left with these two girls. I don't know what the hell happened, but they kicked him out of his car." He paused for a moment and lifted his backward baseball hat from his head before putting it back in place. "I shouldn't drive and I didn't know if you could."

Goddammit. I only had one drink and barely drank the second one I ordered. If there was anyone sober enough to drive here, it was me. I glanced back at the girl with ocean eyes who was staring at me from across the small room.

As much as I wanted to finish what we started, she was just a stranger at the end of the day. These guys were my family and we had to have each other's backs on and off the ice.

I turned back to Wes. "Give me a minute and we'll go get his dumb ass."

"Thanks, Nico."

Leaving the door cracked open, light shined into the

small room as I closed the distance between the girl and me. "I hate to leave like this, but I gotta go."

She smiled up at me. "I get it. You go do whatever you have to do and maybe one day our paths will cross again."

"Let me see your phone," I said to her as I held out my hand.

She raised an eyebrow and pulled it from her clutch. After unlocking the screen, she handed it to me. I took it from her and called my phone from hers.

"There, now you have my number," I told her as I handed it back and slid my hand up to cup the side of her face. "I'm not done with you. Call me if you decide you want to finish this sometime."

I claimed her lips once more with a teasing kiss and grabbed her hand before pulling her out of the room with me. Wes was waiting by the booth and I stopped next to him as I watched her disappear back into the crowd.

"Who was that?"

Shit. I pulled out my phone and saw that I had her number, but I never got her name. A slow smile pulled on my lips.

"I have no idea," I paused as I slid my phone back into my pocket, "but I have every intention of finding out."

Chapter One

Harper

As I rolled out of bed, I checked my phone for the time. I had plenty of time before I had to be at work, so I laid in bed for a moment. It had been three days since the night at the club. After I came out of the storage closet with Nico, I ended up finding Ava who had been looking for me. She was another photographer and I met her when I came for my first interview. We kind of hit it off and she offered to be the one to show me around.

Orchid Beach was a lot different than Boston or Denver but I was slowly getting acclimated to it. The worst part was being alone. I needed a change of scenery after I ended things with my ex. And as soon as the position opened up for the Orchid City Vipers, it seemed like the perfect escape.

I fell in love with Connor in college and stayed with him for far too long. He was drafted into the NHL after we graduated, so we tried to do the long-distance thing. It didn't work for long before I had to end things with him. He seemed like a great guy when I first met him, but after getting into a relationship with him, I realized he wasn't the man I thought he was. After multiple blowout fights and too many hurtful words later, I knew what I had to do.

He was manipulative and when I refused to follow after him, he completely lost it. The night that he threw a glass at my head was the same night I finally ended things. I felt absolutely broken at first. I wasted my time and energy with someone who wasn't good for me. It hurt and I was still healing, but I was finding out that I was much better off without him.

He had other toxic qualities, but I chose to put on my rose-colored glasses when we were together. Now that he was out of my life, I was able to move on. The only problem about being a sports photographer that worked for a professional hockey team… there was going to be a point in my career where I'd most likely see him on the ice.

The only thing I could do is prepare. I wanted him to see what he was missing, but not because I wanted him back. Because I wanted it to be a slap in the face, for him to see that I came out stronger and never needed him.

I allowed myself the luxury of lying in bed for a few more minutes as I scrolled my social media accounts. There was a text from Ava, checking in to see if I wanted to meet up with her before work today. I sent her a response, agreeing to meet her at the coffee shop near the arena before I climbed out of bed and began my routine.

The day passed by quickly and before I knew it, it was time for me to head out. Grabbing all of my equipment, I double-checked my outfit in the mirror and slipped my feet into my sneakers and left my comfortable space to meet Ava.

She was already there when I got to the coffee shop. I held my hand up to wave to her as I walked over to the counter and ordered a latte. The place wasn't busy, which didn't surprise me. It was the middle of the afternoon on a Saturday. The fall air hadn't gone too crisp yet and with the sun still shining, it was a beautiful day outside.

"Are you ready for your first day?" Ava asked as I sat down across from her at the small table by the window. She was wearing an oversized Vipers crewneck and had her dark hair pulled back in a sleek bun.

I took a sip of my latte and nodded. "Yeah. I'm a little nervous but I think I'll feel better after I get this first shoot out of the way."

"That's usually how it goes," she said with a knowing smile. "You'll be fine. I haven't run into anyone who wasn't cool there. Most of the other staff members just leave us alone anyways."

"That's honestly the way I like it."

Ava stared at me for a moment before she leaned forward on her arms. "Okay, we need to talk about the other night. You've been gatekeeping and I need to know what happened."

"I told you, I was dancing with some guy."

She shook her head at me and propped her elbow on the table before dropping her chin to her palm. "I call bullshit. I saw you coming out of the VIP lounge, I just couldn't see who you were with."

Heat crept up my neck and spread across my cheeks. "I don't know who he is. I only got his first name."

"Oh my gosh, look at how you're blushing." Ava's eyes widened as a shocked expression consumed her face. "No way. You hooked up with him in the VIP lounge?"

I cringed and shook my head. "We only kissed… and it was in a storage closet. We got interrupted before it could go any further."

Ava's face cracked and a string of laughter fell from her lips. I couldn't help but laugh along with her after realizing how ridiculous it sounded. Of all the places—a storage closet. That was probably low on my list of places to hook up with someone.

"Damn, girl," she laughed softly and shook her head. "I know you said your ex fucked you up, but he must have done a number on you if you're hooking up with random strangers in closets at the club."

"Dear God, please never say it like that again," I told her as my shoulders sagged in defeat. "That just sounds like I'm a slut."

Ava shook her head. "Absolutely not. You're a goddess and this is your time to shine. Fuck the guys and the relationships. You do you, boo." She paused for a moment and winked. "That asshole doesn't deserve any of your energy. Preserve that shit and save it for someone who earns it."

"You know, I wasn't so sure about you, but you

might not be that bad," I admitted, although I kept my tone light and playful to pass it off as a joke.

Ava checked her watch and rose to her feet as she motioned for me to follow. "Please. I am the best friend you will ever have. You just haven't realized it yet."

Our laughter followed us out of the coffee shop and we parted ways after Ava pulled me in for a hug and promises of seeing each other in literally ten minutes at the arena. Traffic wasn't too bad and I ended up being directly behind her as we showed our cards and pulled into the staff parking lot.

The entire building was already buzzing with energy as we walked through our entrance that led to the media staff room. It wasn't the one where they did the post-game conferences. It was where all of the media staff met and where the photography team would meet up to get our assignments.

As Ava and I walked in, there were already a bunch of people grabbing some food and drinks from a little buffet station they had set up. It surprised me. This was the first professional organization that I had worked for, but I wasn't expecting all of this.

We all gathered in the center of the room and everyone took a seat as Phillip, the head of media, stood in the center to read off our assignments.

"Harper, we're going to have you at the players' entrance and then you'll be at the goal line by the home net for the first period."

I nodded as I wrote that down and looked back over the players list. I had spent last night going through the matchup and highlighting the star players on the team that they would want more photos of. There were two rookies on the team that I needed to make sure I got some shots of. There was a lot of talk about them and the spotlight was on the two of them. Nicolai Cirone and Weston Cole.

The fact that my ex played professional hockey had completely turned me off from following along with the sport. Both of their names were familiar, but that was the most that I knew about them. That and their stats. I guess I would find out what the team really looked like when their skates hit the ice.

After we all broke apart from our meeting, I quickly set up my small station with my laptop and everything ready to go. It was an insane job. Taking thousands of pictures during one twenty-minute period and then having to race back here during the intermission to edit and send some off before taking my next position for the next period. It was a lot. I had done it for some AHL games before, but that was just as a freelancer.

It was high stress and a part of me really enjoyed it. The other part of me wanted something a little more low-key. This was where I was at in life right now and until I had my own business established, this is what work looked like for me.

"Just take a deep breath and everything will be fine," Ava told me as she walked over to my station. "We decide the rest of our assignments usually between the first and second period. Sometimes Phillip will assign them before the game, other times he does it on the fly."

I nodded, taking in any words of encouragement

she could offer me. "I shouldn't feel as anxious as I do right now, but I have a feeling this is going to be crazier than what I'm used to."

Ava smiled at me as she adjusted her own camera bag on her shoulder. "They picked you for a reason. You'll do great."

I smiled back at her before glancing at the watch on my wrist. "I should probably head downstairs and get set up."

"Yeah, they should start heading in within the next twenty minutes or so."

Ava and I parted ways and I took the elevator down to the ice level floor. As the doors slid open, the cold air washed over my skin. A shiver rolled down my spine and I fought the urge to pull my hood up over my head. It wasn't as cold as it was right by the ice, but this floor was definitely the coldest in the building.

I made my way over to where the players' entrance was and I set my bag down on the floor before making myself comfortable. It wasn't the easiest to do, given that the ground was concrete, but I tucked my legs underneath myself and it provided a little comfort and warmth.

My settings were already set up on my camera and I lifted it to my eyes as I took a few practice shots to make sure I had the perfect angle for when they came walking in. Once I was in the right position, I checked my phone for the time and made myself as comfortable as possible.

The first few guys who walked in greeted me and I took my shots of them as they strolled down the hall in their suits. I recognized some of them after checking out the team roster. I offered my name to the ones who asked and they kept on moving.

The guys came in waves and some of them were in pairs. Hockey players were known for being ritualistic creatures and being ones of habit, so I wasn't not surprised when they didn't seem to miss a beat as they all walked past me.

A group of four all came walking in and you could feel the air leave the building as their presence consumed the entire hallway. They were walking in pairs, with two in the front and two behind. I couldn't see the two in the back as they were a few feet behind them and I needed to move to get their pictures too.

I swallowed nervously and continued to take my shots as they were laughing about something. One of the players in the front was wearing a suit that needed to see a dry cleaner to get it pressed. His white dress shirt was wrinkled and so was his suit. His tie was cocked to the side and it made my eye twitch from wanting to fix it for him.

Rising to my feet, I went to move to the side, but the one in the wrinkled suit stepped in front of me. His brow furrowed together and he cocked his head. "I feel like I've seen you somewhere before, but not here." His bright blue eyes were shining as his lips pulled into a smirk. "What's your name?"

"Harper," I told him, my voice soft. "I'm not sure that we would have ever met before. I just moved here."

"I'm Wes," he said as he tucked his hands in the front pockets of his disheveled dress pants. His lips parted and he was about to say something as someone ran directly into his back. "Shit, Cirone," he mumbled as he stepped out of the way.

The air left my lungs in a rush and my eyes widened as his gaze collided with mine. I watched the recognition pass through his expression and my brain tripped over itself as it quickly tried to connect the dots. I didn't make the connection until now. He looked older and different than he did in his rookie picture.

Which is probably why I didn't realize it sooner.

Nico from the club was Nicolai Cirone. One of the star up-and-coming centers for the Orchid City Vipers.

"This is Harper," Wes said to him with a smirk.

Mischief danced in Nico's dark eyes. "Hey, Harper."

I nervously pulled my lip between my teeth and watched his eyes drop down to my mouth. Instinctively, I released it and smiled at him. "Hi, Nico."

Wes lifted an eyebrow at me and I instantly regretted not addressing him by his full name instead. Wes glanced over at Nico. "She's new to the city. Maybe we could show her around sometime…"

His jaw tightened and a shadow passed through his expression before he grabbed Wes's shoulders and swiftly turned him around, giving him a light shove in the back. "Let's go. We're going to be late."

Wes glanced at him over his shoulder with his eyebrows together. "For what, exactly?"

Nico glared at him but didn't bother responding to him as he directed him away from me. Somewhere within those ninety seconds of interaction, my stomach must have fallen onto the ground and my camera wasn't where I needed it to be.

"Shit," I muttered under my breath as a few more players came in. I quickly got back into position and the shutter of the camera clicked as I snapped some shots.

My phone vibrated in my pocket and when I had another short break, I pulled it out. My heart pounded erratically in my chest as I saw I had a text message. It was a number that wasn't saved in my phone, but I knew exactly who it was.

Nico Cirone.

Chapter Two

Nico

> Are you busy after the game?

My mind was still reeling after seeing her. *Harper*. I didn't get her name that night, but now I knew it and it was stuck like glue to the insides of my brain. Wes was rambling on about something beside me, but my eyes were cemented to my phone as I watched the three small bubbles appear and disappear.

"Yo, are you even listening to me?" Wes said as he obnoxiously snapped his fingers in front of my face.

I lifted my gaze to his, my eyes narrowed. "I'm a little busy, if you can't tell."

His eyebrows scrunched together. "Who could possibly be more important than me?"

I snorted and shook my head at Wes just as my phone vibrated in my hand. "Your ego is borderline suffocating."

Wes chuckled. "You'd be lost without me, Cirone."

I rolled my eyes. "You're right. What ever would I do without Weston Cole?"

I'm looking back at my phone as he directed his attention to Lincoln and some of the other guys. They were lost in conversation and I was lost in my mind as I read the message Harper sent back.

HARPER

Who is this?

I bit back a smile and I shook my head to myself. She knew damn well who it was and I wasn't here to play games with her. I wanted answers and I wanted to know when I could see her again.

NICO

Don't fuck with me, pretty girl. You know exactly who this is.

I waited for a few beats and stared down at my phone. Watched as it went from saying delivered to saying read. And those damn bubbles didn't bother to appear. She left me on fucking read.

"Cirone, let's go," Mac called over to me from where the guys were standing with a soccer ball. We always had to do some type of off-ice warm-up before getting on the ice. Soccer was the most recent choice, along with some stretching. They were all already dressed in their warm-up gear and I still had my suit on from when I walked in.

"I'll meet you guys out there in, like, two minutes," I

told Mac as everyone began to file out of the locker room. Mac nodded but didn't speak another word as he followed out after them.

As I rose to my feet, I opened up our message thread again and typed another out to Harper.

NICO

> What do I have to do to get you to meet me somewhere?

I set my phone down and quickly stripped down to my boxers before pulling on my matching t-shirt and a pair of sweatpants. I sat back down on the bench to tie my sneakers as my phone vibrated again.

HARPER

> For starters, you can tell me why you didn't inform me that you played professional hockey for the Orchid City Vipers.

At the time, it didn't feel necessary. A lot of girls acted differently as soon as they found out you played a sport professionally. I didn't know her well enough and I didn't feel comfortable telling her. The same went for her though—she could have easily disclosed what her photography job entailed instead of being vague as fuck about it.

NICO

> Meet me after the game and we can talk.

"Cirone, hurry the fuck up!" I heard Weston's voice from the hall. A sigh escaped me and I shook my head. I don't know what the hell I was thinking or doing. This was a waste of my time. She was just a random hookup and here I was overthinking it all.

The guys were already waiting for me and I left my phone on the bench in an effort to try and forget about the sexy photographer who was in the same goddamn building.

There was something about her that lingered with me after that night at the club. I gave her my number and didn't hear from her. If I wouldn't have ran into her tonight, there was a possibility that I would have been able to forget about her, but not now. Now she was fresh on my brain and right in my damn face.

After we finished our off-ice warm-ups and as I was tying my skates, my phone vibrated from where it was still sitting. My heart pounded erratically and the adrenaline was already fucking with my system. The energy in the room was electric and the boys were ready to go.

I rose to my feet and a message from Harper flashed across the screen. I needed to get ready to go out on the ice, but I found myself staring at the screen and my eyes absorbed her words.

HARPER

I don't know if that's a good idea.

Just as I was about to type a response, Wes grabbed my phone from me and pressed the button on the side to lock the screen. My brow furrowed and I glared at him. My lips parted to ask him what the hell he was thinking, but he silenced me as he shouldered past me to put my phone in my bag.

"Coach will literally take that shit from you like we're in high school and you know it." He stood back in front of me. "Don't fuck around and fuck up, Nico."

As if he heard us talking about him, Coach Anderson walked around the room in his freshly pressed suit, barking orders at everyone. Everyone began to line up and music pounded from the speakers around the arena at the end of the tunnel connected to the locker room.

I stared at my best friend for a moment. "Dude, you're literally always on his shit list."

"Yeah, and it's not a fun place to be, so you're welcome for me trying to save your ass."

"Thanks, bro," I told him as we both got into our respective spots in the line-up. Starting with our goal-tenders, everyone started filing down the tunnel and running onto the ice after grabbing our sticks.

The music was loud, the lights were flashing around, and the entire arena was vibrant. It was a palpable energy. One that you could wrap around your fingertips and string around your body. As I skated across the ice, there was an effortless feeling, almost similar to what I'd imagine flying felt like.

Playing professional hockey was a dream I had always dreamt and now that I had it, I was never going to let it slip away. It was the most exhilarating high, no drug or alcohol could ever come close to touching it. It was deep-seated in my veins and it was something I would never be able to flush out. This was my entire identity and I needed to remind myself that.

We all took shots on the goalie and Wes set me up for a few one-timers as we continued our warm-ups. I could allow myself the luxury of fucking around with Harper, but that was all it could ever be. I would never give any of this up for anyone or anything.

Grabbing the puck with the toe of my stick, I skated around, pushing it along as I headed in the direction of the net. My legs were powering through and I deked to the left and then the right before flicking my wrist and sending the puck top shelf from the right side of the crease. Wolfe, our goalie, didn't have a chance to stop it and he laughed out loud.

"Damn, Cirone." He shook his head as I slid to a stop near him. "Your wrist shot is nasty. I'm ready to see some snipes."

"Let's see what you got," I told him, smiling as I accepted the challenge. I got back into line and we all started skating in rapid succession, firing shots at Wolfe. I wasn't sure how many actual shots on goal I had, but there were only a few that Wolfe managed to block.

He was one of the best goaltenders in the league and a vital asset to our team. He was a few years older than some of the newer guys so he was able to show us a thing or two when it came to playing against some of these other players. Wolfe was a good person to have in your back pocket.

As I finished shooting some shots on goal, I hung

back, letting some of the other guys work Wolfe a little bit. Wes skated over to me and lingered for a moment before saying anything.

"Harper—she's that girl you had in the closet at the club, isn't she?"

Wes's words completely caught me off guard and I whipped my head over to look at him. "What?"

"I knew she looked familiar, I just couldn't figure out why." He paused and smiled. "That explains why you didn't like me talking about showing her around town."

We both directed our gazes back to the net as the boys continued their rounds of making shots. Wes and I both needed to jump in, but he had my attention now.

"I saw her over by the net," Wes said, his voice low. "Are you going to see her again?"

I side-eyed him. "Depends on if she wants to see me or not."

Wes shrugged. "If you end up passing on her, let me know."

My jaw clenched and I looked over at him just as he moved closer over to the boards to do some stretching. The last thing I was going to do was let her fall into Wes's lap. I had a taste of her, but it wasn't enough. I wanted more—enough to satiate my appetite, and then she could do whatever the hell she wanted.

It didn't take but a fraction of a second for me to spot her in her position by the goal line. She was standing over there with her camera lined up through the cutout hole, snapping pictures of our team warming up. A smirk pulled on my lips and I lazily skated over to where she was.

As I neared closer, I turned around and skated backward until my back was against the glass. Glancing over my shoulder, I stopped directly in front of the hole, obscuring her view. It was a dick move, but I wasn't going to let her escape me this easily. I pretended to stretch, even though it was barely a stretch.

"Nico, please move," she raised her voice from where she was sitting and tapped on the glass behind me.

"Don't know what you're talking about," I yelled back to her as one of the pucks came over to me. I received the pass and slid it back over to Wes who raised an eyebrow at me. "I'm just warming up."

"Yeah, I bet you fucking are." She was silent for a breath. "Seriously, I can't see a thing and my job literally depends on this."

"Agree to meet me after the game and I'll leave you alone."

I heard her exasperated sigh and couldn't help but smirk. I had her exactly where I wanted her right now and I was successfully getting her to agree with me.

"Fine. Meet me in the media parking lot."

Without another word, I pushed off the boards and joined the rest of my team as we finished up our warm-ups. I didn't look back in her direction for the last five minutes that I was on the ice, but I could feel her eyes on me. And that was more than enough.

We finished up and all exited the ice so the Zamboni could cut it again and make it fresh before the game began. The boys were buzzing and everyone was hyped. It wasn't long before we were back out there, standing as the woman who sang for our team sang the national anthem. We were playing the Firebirds tonight and they were one of our rivals. We had beat them the past three times we played against them and things were getting relatively tense.

As I skated over to my position for the puck drop, her bright blonde hair caught my attention. She was seated to the right of the net and her camera was positioned through the cutout hole in the glass. My mouth spread into a grin as I bent my knees and placed my stick where I needed it to be for the face-off.

This was going to be a fucking fun night.

I battled my opponent for the puck for a fraction of a second before I was able to get it away from him. Flicking my wrist, I passed it over to Wes, who was already waiting, hanging in the defensive zone. He didn't hesitate to pass it to Mac, who was over on the other side crossing into the neutral zone. The puck was on the ice and the game was on.

We managed to get it into their zone and got two shots on goal, but both were blocked by their goalie. It didn't take long for my first shift to end and my legs were burning but the adrenaline quickly washed over me. I dropped down onto the bench next to Wes and we both grabbed our bottles and drank from them as we watched the game continue.

"What was that with Harper?" Wes asked me out of nowhere. "I saw the two of you talking about something."

I glanced over at him with my gaze slicing through his. "I'm going to tell you one time and this is the last fucking time." My voice was as sharp as ice. He was my best friend but I knew how Wes operated. He ran through girls like it was his job. "Forget her name and stay away from her."

Wes raised his eyebrows at me. "I take it that you're not passing on her then?"

An exasperated sigh escaped me. I didn't know what the hell I was really doing, but I knew that I didn't want Wes to get any ideas about her. Our conversation was interrupted as Lincoln was checked into the boards by us. He lost his footing momentarily, but quickly recovered before skating after the asshole who slammed into him.

A few of the guys skated over for a line change. Without another word to Wes, I hopped over the boards, even though it wasn't my shift, and sped across the ice, chasing after the puck and the pack of players. As I skated into their zone, Lincoln slid the puck to me. I received the pass and weaved through two of their players before sniping the small spot between the goalie's leg and his stick.

The bull horn sounded throughout the building and it echoed as our fans cheered loudly. The boys on the bench were slapping their sticks against the boards and I went for a different celly this time, dropping to one knee as I pointed my stick toward Harper from across the ice. The guys on the ice all skated over to me and when I got over to the bench, the guys had their hands out and I bumped my glove against each of theirs.

Coach Anderson looked less than amused that I was on the ice when the rest of my line was still on the bench.

I may have scored a goal, but there was definitely going to be hell to pay for that stunt.

I had a feeling it would be worth it in the end.

Chapter Three

Harper

The entire night flew by faster than I had expected. It was a complete whirlwind and I would be lying if I said that it didn't leave me feeling completely exhausted. During the periods, I was busy trying to capture as many shots as possible and during the intermissions, I was swamped with editing hundreds of images to send off to the media team.

They liked to have images to share on social media and the various websites during the game, so it was essential that we had them edited and sent over while the action was happening. We got our assignments for the rest of the game after the first period and they had me positioned on the glass for everything.

It was hard to ignore Nico Cirone and his presence. He dominated the game and made his place on the ice well known. It was impossible to deny that he was an extremely talented player and he skated with purpose. He still had a lot to lose and couldn't miss a beat with proving himself.

Between him and Weston Cole, they ran most of the plays. It was exhilarating to watch, but I also had to be mindful while shooting that I couldn't just have a million pictures of the two of them. They weren't the only players who mattered on the team and even though Nico had infiltrated my mind and shook things up, I had to push him from my thoughts as much as possible during the game.

I was closing my laptop and packing my things away when Ava found me by my station. She strode over with a huge smile on her face.

"Girl, you killed it tonight!" She adjusted her bag on her shoulder. "Did you check the Instagram account? They used your shot from the game-winning goal on it."

My eyes widened and my heart pounded erratically in my chest. With it being my first day on the job, it was not what I was expecting to hear at all. "Are you serious?"

Ava showed me her phone and, lo and behold, there was the photo I took of Mac O'Reilly scoring on the Firebird's goalie during the last ten seconds of the game. "This calls for a celebration, girl. Let's go out!"

I gave her a small smile. "I have something else that I have to do tonight, but can we celebrate tomorrow night instead?"

"Absolutely," Ava said with a smile as she nodded. "Tomorrow night. I'll text you in the morning after I figure out what trouble we can get into."

I laughed softly and shrugged. "I'm not usually one

for trouble but fuck it. I need some excitement in my life."

"Good answer."

Ava pulled me in for a quick hug with a promise of talking in the morning before we parted ways. She disappeared from the media room before I did and part of that was because I was so nervous to walk out to my car.

I knew that Nico would be out there waiting for me and I wasn't sure I was ready to face him yet.

I couldn't hang out in here forever and after giving myself a ten-minute long pep talk in the bathroom, I finally sucked it up and headed out to the parking lot. Most of the members from the media team had already left and there were only a handful of cars remaining.

As I walked alone, I spotted my car where I had left it in its spot and parked right next to it was Nico's sleek Mercedes Benz. He was leaning against the front of his car wearing a pair of gray sweatpants and a black Vipers hoodie. His phone illuminated his face and as I neared closer, he lifted his head as he spotted me.

Nico dropped his phone and tucked it into the front pocket of his sweatpants as he pushed away from the front of his car. My stomach did a somersault as I approached him and the nervousness was swirling around in my veins again.

"Hey," he said, his voice soft and warm as he smiled at me. "How did your night go?"

His question caught me off guard with the simplicity of it. I shifted my weight nervously. "It went well. It was pretty intense and exhilarating at the same time."

Nico flashed his white teeth at me and my stomach did a weird flutter thing that I instantly wanted to shut off. This man almost had me naked a few days ago and his tongue was inside my mouth. What the hell was this life I was living?

"I'm really glad to hear that." He paused for a breath. "I would apologize for blocking your view during warm-ups, but it would be a lie. I needed to see you again and it worked out in my favor."

I almost choked on my breath as he spoke the words. His arrogance wasn't as evident the first night I met him. He definitely exuded confidence, but goddamn. This was a different side of him and I wasn't sure if I was turned on or wanted to slap him.

"Ah, so you're all about yourself and getting what you want?"

Mischief danced in his irises and he shrugged. "I'm used to getting what I want."

I tilted my head to the side as I set my camera and laptop bags on the hood of my car. "Is that why you didn't tell me that you were a professional hockey player?"

Nico raised an eyebrow at me. "Quite the contrary. If I tell women that, it's usually a done deal that they're coming home with me." His tongue slid out as he wet his lips. "I wanted you to want me for me, not because of my status."

"Are you always this forward with people?"

A chuckle vibrated from his chest and I swear I felt it in between my legs. Heat crept up my neck and quickly made its way across my cheeks as I clenched my thighs together.

His lips twitched. "You're blushing."

"No, I'm not," I retorted as I ducked my head and grabbed my bags.

As I lifted them into the air, Nico wrapped his hand around mine and took them from me. My gaze collided with his and he stared down at me with a fire burning in his irises.

"I like how you look when you blush, knowing I'm the one who put that color in your cheeks."

My breath caught in my throat and my heart pounded erratically against my rib cage as I tried to regain my composure. There was no reason for him to be having this effect on me. We hooked up one night, if you even want to call it that.

If his friend hadn't interrupted us that night, we would have definitely had sex. That was in the exact direction we were heading, but it didn't happen. We had a moment and it should be left at just that.

Nico walks himself over to the passenger's side of my car and sets my bags inside before making his way back over to me. Part of me knows I should have stopped him but his forwardness has me feeling like I have vertigo.

"What did you want to meet up to talk about?" I asked him as he stopped in front of me.

The look in his eyes was indistinguishable and the tension between us was palpable. The air was electric and I was afraid I was going to get shocked if I dared to reach out and touch it between my fingertips.

"I wanted to see you again."

The words fell from his lips with no hesitation. He didn't say it with a question, he wasn't asking if he could see me again. He was telling me what he wanted and Nico already made it clear that Nico Cirone gets what he wants.

"Well, I'm here, and honestly, I'm exhausted," I told him as I attempted to brush away the effect he was having on me. It could be my own little secret and not one that I needed him to know about. "So, if you wanted to talk, I'd get to it now."

He tucked his hands in the front pockets of his pants and his expression softened as his eyes searched mine. "I was surprised to see you when I got here today. You've been on my mind since the night at the club and I was literally going to give you another day or two to call me before I called you."

"I was equally surprised," I reminded him. "I suppose we both could have told each other more about our jobs, but we didn't really leave a lot of room for conversation."

This earned a smirk from him. "No, we didn't, did we?" His wavy dark hair poked out from the top of his hood that was pulled up around his head and I remember how soft it was. How it felt like silk between my fingers. "I meant what I said that night."

I swallowed roughly as his words from that night played over in my head. His gaze was glued to mine and the way he was staring at me had me ready to climb into the back seat of his car.

"I wasn't done with you that night and I'm not done with you now."

Cue melting into a puddle on the ground around his feet.

My chest expanded as I inhaled deeply and slowly let out the breath in my lungs. "This changes things now, Nico. We both work for the same organization. You know how their policies are regarding fraternizing with other staff."

His jaw tightened and he glowered at me. "Fuck the policies, Harper. You don't strike me as someone who follows the rules."

"Maybe not, but I need this job."

His face relaxed and he took a step toward me. "Can I tell you a secret?"

My tongue stuck to the roof of my mouth like I had a mouthful of peanut butter. He was so close I could smell the scent of his body wash from the showers inside the locker rooms. I didn't dare speak a word, but stupidly nodded instead.

"Tonight was literally the best game I played since they moved me up from the farm team." He paused for a beat and I counted two erratic heartbeats in my chest before his beautiful lips parted again. "I think I found my good luck charm for the season and I'm not giving that up."

I stare at him for a moment in disbelief. "You can't be serious."

Hockey players were known for their superstitions and ritualistic behavior. If something worked for one game as a good luck charm, that was the be-all and end-all until it didn't work anymore.

"Do I look like I'm joking?" he said with a dead serious look on his face. "I need you around, Harper. And I think I can help you too. Kind of like a mutual trade-off."

My brows pinched together and I eyed him skeptically. "What are you proposing, Cirone?"

"You wanted me to erase the memories of your ex," he reminded me from the night in the club, and I instantly blushed again. "Let me replace every bad fucking memory of him. I'm not going to be your rebound, but more like your stepping stone to getting back into the game."

"Did you not hear a single word I said about the policy against fraternizing?" I argued with a frustrated sigh. "If we get caught doing anything together, I would most likely lose my job."

Nico stared at me. "So, we don't get caught."

"I'm not in the habit of sleeping around."

He smirked and shrugged. "It's not sleeping around if you're sleeping with the same person."

"I cannot believe we're seriously having this conversation right now," I muttered under my breath as I shook my head. "Look, I'm flattered and appreciate your forwardness, I guess?" I shook my head again. "This is beyond bizarre and I think I'm just going to go home now."

Nico stepped out of my way without arguing. Something lingered in his gaze as he watched me walk to the driver's side door and pull it open. "Think about it, but don't take too long." He fell silent for a second, his gaze colliding with mine just as I was about to lower myself into my seat. "Have a good night, Harper."

My stomach was in my throat as I dropped down and quickly closed the door behind me. I didn't bother looking at him again, but I could feel his eyes watching me from where he stood by his car.

And as I pulled out of the parking lot, my phone vibrated in my bag. I paused at the exit, pulling it out as I unlocked my phone and read the message that had come through.

NICO

Don't forget, Harper... I get what I want.

I quickly locked my screen and tossed it onto the seat beside me as a rush of adrenaline raced through my veins. There was no way I could get away from him now. My mind couldn't even fully process what just happened, but there was one thing I knew for sure.

I was officially fucked by Nico Cirone and he hadn't even fully touched me yet.

Chapter Four

Nico

I had no intention of being as forward as I was with Harper. It was one of those situations that you find yourself going too far in and there was literally no turning back. Once I had started, I felt like I had to follow through, even if it meant pushing her away. I wasn't sure if that was truly the case or if I had just confused her that much.

Either way—she left me without an answer and I had no intention of accepting that.

She had just become my new obsession.

It had been almost a week since I had run into Harper at the Orchid Beach Arena and I hadn't heard from her since. I kept glancing down at my phone, waiting for it to vibrate. It had become a recent habit and it made my eye twitch when I realized how ridiculous this was becoming.

We were flying home later tonight and had a home game in two days. After being on the road for three straight games, I was ready to be back at my apartment. But more importantly, I was ready to see Harper again.

"You keep looking at your phone like it's a bomb that's about to detonate," Wes mused out loud as he sat across from me at our table. We came to get dinner at a restaurant not far from the airport before leaving.

I rolled my eyes. "No, I don't."

"Sure you do," he argued before taking a sip of his drink. "You've been doing it for days now. I can't tell if you're waiting for good news or bad."

I raised an eyebrow at him. None of the other guys were paying attention to us and for that, I was extremely grateful. "I'm not waiting for either."

Wes mimicked my expression. "So, it's more of a who then instead of a what." He paused as an amused smirk played on his lips. "It's the photographer, isn't it? Harper?"

My eyes widened slightly and I gave him a murderous glare. "Dude, shut up about her."

He fought back a laugh and silenced himself as he took another sip of his beer. "That's what I thought."

"No one can know about that shit at the club and you do not know how to keep your mouth closed." I paused for a moment, dropping my voice lower. "If I want any chance of anything else happening with her, I can't have anyone knowing."

Realization finally dawned over Wes's expression and I swore, sometimes it really took him a few moments before he caught up. I suppose too many blows to the head would do that to you.

"Ah, shit, her job with the organization," he said

with his voice as low as mine. "There has to be some kind of a loophole or a work-around."

I shrugged as I took a swig of my own beer. "Trust me, I already have a plan, because I need her."

"Damn, dude, you plan on wifing her up this quickly too?"

My nostrils flared as I let out an exasperated sigh. "It's not completely like that. Just hear me out... I need her around to play like I did the other night."

Wes gave me a look like I was insane, but it tracked. I didn't play terribly while we were on the road, but I didn't play like I did that night she was at the game. It wasn't like I had anything to prove to her, so it had to be another good luck charm sent to me from the universe.

"What about Ballsy?"

I laughed out loud at the thought of someone overhearing us and what their thoughts might be. To anyone that wasn't seated at our table, our conversation would have sounded like some off-the-wall shit.

"Ballsy is one thing I will never, ever give up, so don't worry. She's not a threat to him."

Wes laughed along with me. "Oh, thank God. I don't know what we would do if you threw out that ball of tape." He grabbed the pitcher of beer from the center of the table and filled up his glass. "What version of Ballsy is this one anyways?"

Wes knew the history behind Ballsy, but it had become a bit of a joke between the two of us. No one knew the history behind it but him. One drunken night, I broke down after he grilled me about the damn ball of tape and I told him the truth. The connection to my late mother.

Ballsy made an appearance every season and that habit was never going anywhere.

"I honestly don't even know. I stopped counting after it was Ballsy the tenth."

Mac cleared his throat from where he was sitting next to Wes and we both glanced over at him. "Sometimes I really wonder about the two of you and question the stability of your mental health."

"If you need to worry about either of us, it would be him," I joked, motioning to Wes.

Wes barked out a laugh. "Says the guy who has a ball of tape THAT HE NAMED."

"Oh, yeah, I heard about that," Mac said with his curiosity now piqued. "This is something I have to see sometime."

"It truly is a work of art," I tell him with the smile of a proud parent on my face. "I have a picture of the one from last season, if you want to see it."

I picked up my phone to scroll through my photos to find one to show him, when it vibrated in my hand. Heat instantly crept up my neck, warming my entire body, and I locked my screen before tucking it back into my pocket.

"Actually, I don't have any good ones. I'll have to find them another time."

Mac shrugged and didn't seem to really care, while Wes raised an eyebrow at me. I narrowed my eyes at him in warning and he gave me a nod before diving into a conversation with Mac.

Lincoln stood up from his seat and knocked on the table to get everyone's attention. "Coach wants us ready to leave in, like, ten minutes, so be ready, boys."

A few of the guys grumbled, but I think a majority of us were just ready to get back to our home city. I sat back quietly in my seat as I eased away from any of the conversations and pulled my phone back out of my pocket to check my messages.

There she was… finally responding.

HARPER

Hey.

That was it. Simplistic, yet highly cryptic.

NICO

Hey yourself.

She was severely mistaken if she thought this was how I played. She should have known from the other night that I wasn't one to beat around the bush. I was straight up with her and I wasn't sure I should expect the same from her in return.

HARPER

So, I was thinking about what you said the other night and I don't see how it is going to work out.

Ah, there it was. The answer that I was half expecting, but not the one I was wanting to hear.

NICO

And why is that?

My mother taught me better. She raised me to be a respectful gentleman. I would at least be decent enough to show Harper that. I would never push her—or anyone—into something they didn't want.

> **HARPER**
> It's just too risky. I have too much to lose.

So, she wasn't saying she didn't want to. It was more a matter of we couldn't because of what could happen.

> **NICO**
> What if I told you that no one would ever find out?

> **HARPER**
> Someone always finds out, Nico.

I shook my head at my phone and tucked it into my pocket as everyone got up from the table. We had a bus waiting out front to take us to the airport where we would board our team's jet and head back to Orchid Beach. I followed Wes out of the restaurant and my phone was burning a hole in my pocket.

The last words that Harper sent continued to plague my mind until we were all filing onto the jet and taking our seats. Some of the guys had fallen into comfortable conversation and a few were already half asleep. Wes was reading a romance novel and I wasn't even about to approach that subject.

Instead, I pulled out my phone and opened up the message thread between Harper and me. She wasn't wrong with her statement. In most cases, that was what happened. Things always got out and then you were fucked.

What Harper didn't know was I wouldn't tell a single soul, not even Wes. If I could prevent anyone from finding out, that was what I would do. She didn't understand the weight we put on good luck charms.

I needed her around, even if she didn't want to take me up on my offer.

NICO

That's where you're wrong, love. I plan on keeping things between us quiet but have no intention of you being quiet.

HARPER

Are you always so sure of yourself?

A smile pulled on my lips and I stared down at my phone as the pilot drove the jet onto the runway. I had approximately a minute before we would be in the air and needed to put my phone on airplane mode.

NICO

How else do you think I stay on top?

HARPER

You're a top all right...

Damn. She made my dick hard with one sentence.

Her response was not what I had expected. I had definitely underestimated her and now I didn't feel as badly about coming on as strongly as I did. I wasn't here to fuck around. Not in the sense of leaving things open to her interpretation. I knew what I wanted and was simply making sure she knew it too.

NICO

You want to play, love? I can show you how good it feels to win.

Three small bubbles popped up and disappeared as she typed and deleted a response. My heart pounded against my rib cage and excitement rattled my system as I waited in limbo for her response.

"Cirone, we're about to take off. Phone."

Our coach made me feel like I was back in high school all over again as he scolded me for having my phone out. A sigh escaped me as I closed out of the message thread. I quickly switched it over to airplane mode and slid it back into my pocket.

I caught Wes looking at me from where he was sitting. A smirk played on his lips and he cocked an eyebrow.

I shook my head at him. "Just don't."

I had half a hard-on and felt awkward as hell as I attempted to adjust myself in my seat with my best friend staring at me the way he was.

"I didn't say anything," Wes said as he feigned innocence and held up the novel he was reading. "I'm just over here minding my own business."

"Sure you are," I threw back at him as a laugh escaped me. "You have a habit of making everyone's business your own."

Wes gave me the middle finger as he laughed along before he got back to whatever the hell it was he was reading. Shaking my head, I settled back in my seat, feeling the plane lift into the air as I rested my head against the window.

I hated that I would have to wait until we touched down to read Harper's response, but good things took time.

And I planned on having the best fucking time with her.

Chapter Five

Harper

"You're quiet today," Ava said as we both sat down at the table in the coffee shop. It had become our little thing before work. We would meet here, if neither of us had anything going on, and grab some coffee before we had to head to the arena.

I hadn't told Ava anything about Nico. All she knew was about some random guy at the club, but I never told her the truth about who it really was. I also never disclosed the fact that he played professional hockey for the same team that we worked for.

It wasn't that I didn't trust Ava. She was the only friend I really made since moving to Orchid Beach. She hadn't given me a reason not to trust her, but at the same time, I still found myself hesitant. If I let her in on anything that had to do with Nico, how would I know that she wouldn't end up saying something to someone?

It was really hard to make that judgment when you didn't know someone completely.

And on the other hand—it's not like there was anything real going on between Nico and I. Some harmless flirting and whatnot after our run-in at the club. He had propositioned me and I didn't take the bait. No harm, no foul. Neither of us could realistically get in trouble for what had happened between us so far.

I knew the limitations and knew where it had to be cut off. It could never progress any further than it already had and I planned on telling Nico that... eventually. I never responded to his last text two nights ago. Part of me knew that I should have shut that down immediately, yet I couldn't bring myself to do it.

Chances were, I would end up seeing him tonight, whether it was on or off the ice.

Then I would tell him the truth.

I shrugged as I took a sip of my latte. "I just didn't sleep very well last night. I woke up late and then the gym was so busy." I paused for a second and let out a sigh. "I know, they're all stupid problems. I'm just ready to get tonight over with and go to bed."

"Girl, I get it completely. We all have shit days and you're allowed to have one." She smiled at me, before pulling out a small compact mirror and a tube of lip gloss. "Just breathe in the good and exhale the bad. Tonight will be amazing, you will be amazing and then you'll get to go home."

I stared at Ava, a little taken aback by her sudden yogi attitude. "Are you going through some type of spiritual awakening?"

It was Ava's turn to sigh. "Ryan has been on this yoga, like meditation, manifesting kick. I'm not against it at all—it really helps my mindset—but sometimes I can't help but wonder if it's all a crock of shit."

I tried really hard not to laugh, but I couldn't stop the string of laughter from falling from my lips. Ava laughed along and gave me the middle finger. "I'm sorry, I shouldn't laugh. I just can't picture Ryan doing that."

Ava's boyfriend really was a nice, laid-back, quiet guy. He also kind of freaked me out sometimes. He was smart—like *smart* smart, genius level smart. There was nothing bad about the guy. He had just made jokes about hacking into stuff and with his dry humor, it was hard to tell if he was serious or not.

Which all made it hard to picture him sitting with his feet together and his eyes closed as he let out an "om".

"Next thing you know, he's going to be dragging me along to a fucking ayahuasca retreat or something." Ava shook her head and rolled her eyes. "I love the guy and I've done my fair share of mushrooms, but I'm not trying to experience ego death. That might literally kill me."

My eyes widened. I had heard about people doing those retreats. Supposedly, it was one of the most humbling, life-changing experiences ever. It also sounded like pure hell and something I would never want to experience either.

"Please tell me he didn't say anything about doing one."

"Not yet, girl," Ava said with a soft laugh. "I don't think he's far away from suggesting it, though."

"I'll pray for you," I joked as we both laughed.

"I'm going to need the whole damn church praying for me."

————

When we got to the media room at the stadium, it was a repeat of the last time. Our assignments were handed out and this time we received them for the entire game. It gave me some peace knowing where I was expected to be during the period of play. I frowned as I looked over where they wanted me.

I was expected to take pictures from the players' entrance again and during the press release afterward. Thankfully, my game assignments were opposite corners by the net that we would shoot on twice and one by our net. What it essentially meant was there would be no possible way to avoid running into Nico Cirone.

So, this would be a fun night for sure.

After setting up my station, I headed down to the ice level floor and set up by the players' entrance. It wouldn't be long before they would all come strolling in. I adjusted my camera settings and made myself comfortable on the concrete floor and did a few practice shots.

As the guys started to come in, I snapped shots of each one. They all greeted me, remembering me from the last game. I wondered if this was where Phillip would have me most games. The guys seemed to appreciate the familiar face and a few even asked how I was doing and what my name was.

Until the two who definitely knew my name came walking in.

This time they were alone. Just Nico and Wes. They were talking about something and Weston was getting animated with his hands, half skipping along. He reminded me of a little kid with how his face lit up when he talked. And the fact that his entire outfit was wrinkled again.

My mouth went dry as Nico looked directly at the camera and winked at me. He looked just as good as he always did and I wanted to slap myself out of the trance I found myself in.

"Hey, Harper," he said as the two of them stopped to the right of me. No one else was behind them so there was no excuse for me still holding my camera up. I swallowed roughly and lowered it to my lap as I looked up at the two of them.

"Hey, Nico," I replied and looked to his friend and nodded. "Wes."

"We really missed you while we were away," Wes said with a sad smile and puppy dog eyes. "You should come on the road with us next time."

I practically choked on my own saliva. "Yeah, I don't know. I'd have to talk to Phillip. I'm pretty sure they usually send the more seasoned photographers on the road."

"I stalked your social media. They'd be stupid not to send you."

Nico whipped his head to look at him. "You did what?"

"Wait, you did?" I asked at the same time.

Wes glanced sheepishly between the two of us. "I mean, I was curious. You take really good pictures. Just try a little harder to get my better side when you see me on the ice." He smirked as he swept his hand along the right side of his jaw. "See ya later, Harp." He nodded at me before he continued to walk, purposely leaving Nico and I alone.

Silence encapsulated us as Nico watched Wes until he was out of sight. My heart pounded and I could see the sound of the blood rushing through my veins. My stomach did a flip and a twinge of excitement slid down my spine.

No one was around. It was just the two of us and Nico Cirone was staring down at me as waves crashed against the shores of his ocean eyes. I hated the way he was looking at me. The visceral effect that it had on me.

How the hell was I ever going to be able to ignore this man if he looked at me like this every time we were near each other?

"You never answered my text."

My breath caught in my throat. I nervously shifted my weight as I went over what I wanted to say in my mind. I was not prepared to have this conversation right now. "I figured it would be better to talk about it in person."

Nico lifted an eyebrow. "Color me curious. Go ahead, love. Don't be shy."

I cleared my throat. "I think we need to just let all of

this go." Nico stared at me, but he remained silent. I had no idea where I was going with this, but it was my chance to get out of this situation. "We had our moment that one night and I think it's best if we just leave it at that. That time has passed and you know, given our circumstances, things are a little different now."

His gaze lingered. Nothing about his expression changed. It was quite blank, void of any emotion, although his eyes painted a picture I couldn't quite decipher. "I see."

"I know what you said about being a good luck charm and you know, I'm still here, so there's always that."

"Hmm," he mused and nodded. He shoved his hands in the front pockets of his dress pants, but he didn't move from where he was standing. Even though he was above me, he was too close. Yet a part of me wanted him closer. "I suppose you're right."

His reaction threw me off-balance and I cocked my head as I continued to look up at him. "That's it? You're okay with that?" I didn't expect him to just agree like that, not after everything he had already said to me. There was a part of me that couldn't help but be annoyed with him in this moment.

Nico scowled. "What were you expecting? Me to beg you to reconsider? Believe it or not, love, I'm a rather agreeable person."

"I thought you get what you want."

A low chuckle rumbled in his chest. "Oh, I do. Just because I'm agreeing with you doesn't mean I won't get what I want in the end." He let out a sigh and his eyes softened a bit. "I play the long game, love. I might move quickly on the ice, but I treat life like a marathon."

"So, you're verbally agreeing with me, but in your mind, you don't agree at all?" I blinked twice as he stood there in silence.

I didn't believe him at all in this moment. He could appear as agreeable as he wanted, but his words just told a different story. They showed a different angle. He wasn't just agreeing and moving on from the arrangement he proposed. He was simply lying in wait, while planning his next move.

Nico Cirone was calculated. Forward and a tad abrasive, but he didn't strike without a plan in place.

The door from the entrance opened and closed and Nico glanced over his shoulder before looking back at me. His lips slowly crept upward and he winked. "Better get back to work, Harper. Don't want you breaking any rules and missing out on any shots."

Heat crept up my neck and quickly spread across my cheeks as I directed my gaze away from him. As I lifted my camera back in front of my face and began to press the shutter button, Nico disappeared in the direction of the locker rooms.

He wasn't going to make this easy at all.

And I wasn't sure just how long I would be able to keep resisting him.

Chapter Six

Nico

We were deep into the second period with only three minutes left and I felt like I was on fire. I already had four points for the game—two goals and two assists. It was looking to be a complete shutout. Wolfe brought his A game. Literally everyone on our team was playing the best version of themselves.

It had to be because of Harper.

There was no other explanation.

The ref called an icing after Lincoln tossed the puck back into our zone. We headed down to the defensive zone for a face-off and I caught sight of Harper with her face hidden behind her camera. A smile pulled on my lips and I got into my position with my stick ready to fight.

"Sup Cirone?" The player next to me nodded his head as I met his gaze. Alexander Stone. We played college hockey together and it had been a minute since I last saw him.

"Stone," I replied with a clipped tone as I grew impatient waiting for the ref to drop the puck. Stone was known for chirping and he was a dickhead. I kept my distance from him, even though we played on the same team.

"You look just as pretty as you always have."

I side-eyed him. "Fuck off, Stone."

"What?" He laughed. "You've always been known for being the pretty boy who stays wheelin' chicks. Speaking of—you think you can hook me up with one while I'm in town? My dick could use a good sucking, unless you'd rather wrap those pretty lips around it instead."

This was Alexander Stone. A fucking pig with no respect for anyone. This was also the exact reason why he ended up in fights during most games he played. He didn't know how to stay in his own lane.

It was one thing to chirp and talk shit during a game, but he always took it too far.

Just as the ref dropped the puck, Stone threw his shoulder into mine instead of even bothering to battle for the black piece of rubber. I managed to get it anyway and tossed it to Lincoln before getting in Stone's face.

"What the fuck was that?"

"Just seeing if you're still a fragile little bitch," he laughed out loud, winking before he started to skate away. "You took that hit pretty well."

It wasn't often that I got into fights, but something about the way he was talking was working under my skin. I knew that this was to be expected. I could always out-skate him and he was jealous of how I played compared to him. Stone had always been an envious person and let it get the better of him.

Although, I wasn't sure there was anything better about him.

I skated after him as we headed into the neutral zone and slashed my stick against the side of his calves. It was a dirty move and one I didn't usually pull, but I was fucking annoyed with him. Stone had a habit of pushing people to this point and it wasn't the first time we ended up in a fight.

He spun around, his eyes wild, and he threw his gloves onto the ice before squaring up with me. A sinister smirk formed on his face. I would definitely get a penalty for slashing, but he was the one who threw his mitts first. All I was doing was defending myself.

His fist hit the side of my head, rattling my brain a bit. I reached out, grabbing the collar of his jersey while trying to keep myself upright. Curling my other hand into a fist, I drove it into the side of his face. The shield of his helmet cut through the back of my hand. I ignored the pain and the blood while we took turns delivering blows to each other's faces.

"Not so pretty anymore, Cirone," Stone sneered with a smirk. I drove all of my body weight into him, knocking him down onto the ice. I followed along with him, landing on top of him.

It wasn't long before one of the refs was lifting me away and two were between us, keeping us separated. I tasted blood on my tongue as I ran it over the cut on my lip.

"Good fight, Nico. I see you learned how to throw a harder punch." He smiled at me with a mouthful of blood before he started talking shit to the ref. That was how Alexander Stone operated. And I simply shook my head as more distance was put between us.

We both ended up in the penalty box and he was still chirping from where he was sitting. Thankfully, the numerous walls of glass between us were making it harder to understand the shit that was spewing from his lips. He wasn't even talking about me at this point.

Stone was one of those guys who'd had one too many concussions. It made you question if he was even living in the same reality as the rest of the planet. Head injuries were no joke and I wouldn't be surprised if his next one would end up being his last and what would have him out of the league.

It was a shame because he was a decent player. He just had a big mouth and talked a lot of shit. He only talked shit to his own teammates during practices and scrimmage games. Other than that, he was a ride or die team player. Either way, I still didn't like him and I probably never would.

The buzzer sounded throughout the arena as the second stanza had come to an end. I was let out of the box and skated over to the door by our team's bench. Everyone else was already making their way down the tunnel and just as I stepped through the door, I glanced over, catching Harper's gaze from where she was standing. She was making her way up the stairs, most likely to head back to the media room.

The expression on her face looked less than amused

and she shook her head at me in disapproval. My eyebrows scrunched together in confusion from the look she was giving me. I wanted to close the distance between us. I wanted to pluck the thoughts from her mind. Instead, she ducked her head and continued to walk up the stairs toward the concourse.

Mac pressed his gloved hands against the middle of my back, giving me a slight shove. "Let's go, Cirone."

I didn't argue with him. Instead, I began the trek down the tunnel to the locker room. Mac and I were the last two to walk in. Mac brushed past me and took a seat on the bench. I kind of lingered for a moment before I sat down. Wes slid over to me with a look of curiosity.

"You an enforcer now?" Weston challenged me with his voice low. "What happened out there?"

I shrugged with a look of indifference as I attempted to brush it off. "You know Stone. He's just a fucking asshole."

"Don't give him a reaction. You know that's all he's looking for."

"Yeah, I know," I nodded along in agreement. "I don't know what came over me. Usually the shit he says just rolls off but for some reason he really got under my skin."

I wasn't about to relay the vulgar things that Stone said to me. It was one thing to chirp and talk shit, but it was another to keep it more lighthearted. Stone was just mean-spirited and Wes was right. I couldn't let it get to me. It was already over and what was done was done.

Even though I would have to face him again in the third period, the fight was over.

In reality, it wasn't even the fight that was weighing on my mind. It was the way Harper looked at me. Almost like she was disappointed in me. I couldn't shake the feeling that slid down my spine. I felt like I did something to offend her and I didn't like how it was settling in my bones. I couldn't fully explain it, but I knew I was only using the fight with Alexander to block thoughts of Harper from my brain.

"I saw your good luck charm was here tonight," Wes said, breaking through my thoughts with his quiet voice. "You're grinding hard tonight and I think your theory might be pretty solid. You have the evidence to back it up."

"She doesn't want anything to do with me, man."

Wes raised an eyebrow. "Did she tell you that?"

I grabbed a bottle and squirted some water into my mouth. "She thinks the moment between us has passed. It's too risky, so she says, for us to even see each other."

"Ah." Wes nodded like he suddenly had the answers he was looking for. "That explains the fight. You're trying to work out the shit in your head."

I stared at him for a moment. "Are you a player on the team or our shrink? Stop overanalyzing me, Cole."

"Can I give you a piece of advice?"

"No."

Wes laughed. "Well, you're getting it anyways. Don't give up on her yet. Maybe try to do something normal like take her out to dinner or some shit. Be her friend, get to know her."

"I never said that I didn't want to do any of that." I narrowed my eyes at him. "I don't want to push her away. I'm trying to play it smart."

He shrugged. "Well, either you push her away or toward you. Where you stand right now, I don't think you have much to lose."

I mulled over Wes's words and before I knew it, it was time for us to head back out to the ice. I pushed it all to the farthest corner of my mind and played my ass off. We ended up with a shutout and the boys were on a whole different level with their energy. Everyone wanted to go out and celebrate.

I just wanted to go home.

The guys all made plans to meet up at a local bar and I told them that I would maybe stop by. I headed out alone and there weren't very many cars left in the parking lot. After pulling out and making my way around the stadium, I slowed down while passing the staff parking lot.

Harper's car was still there and I couldn't stop myself as I pulled in and parked next to her. It was stupid and I knew it, but I couldn't help myself. I wanted to see her—I needed to see her. After everything tonight, she was the only one I really wanted to talk to.

I waited until I saw her exiting the building before getting out of my car. Her steps faltered for a moment as she crossed the parking lot, undoubtedly noticing my car sitting next to hers. As I stepped around the front of my vehicle, she gave me a small nod and put her stuff on her passenger's seat before walking over to me.

"Nico," she said softly, yet her expression was filled with a look of questioning and hesitation. "What are you doing out here?"

I shifted my weight on my feet and tucked my hands into the front pocket of my hoodie. "I was waiting for you."

Harper stared at me for a moment as she wrapped her arms around herself to block out the cool evening breeze. "Why?"

Her cheeks were tinted pink and wisps of her blonde hair blew across her face. Instinctively, I reached out and brushed them away, tucking them behind her ears. I heard the sharp intake of her breath as the tips of my fingers grazed her soft skin. Harper's eyes bounced back and forth between my own.

I shrugged as I pulled my hand away. "I don't know. I just felt like I needed to after I saw you earlier."

Her expression softened and she took a hesitant step closer to me. She lifted her hand to cup the side of my face and her gaze dropped to my lips as she gently touched the cut in my lip.

"I didn't like seeing you fight tonight," she breathed, her voice barely audible. Her touch was tender and her gaze collided with mine as she lifted her eyes. "What happened out there? Are you okay?"

"I'm fine," I told her, reaching up to wrap my hand around her wrist. I meant to pull her away from my face, but instead I found myself wanting to pull her closer. "Just normal stuff that happens on the ice."

Her throat bobbed. "I get that. I'm not a stranger to

watching the fights. I just don't want to see you get hurt."

Her words slid through my veins, warming my body as they flowed from her lips. I stared down at her, the corners of my mouth twitching. "I didn't know you cared."

"I never said I cared," she grumbled as I dropped my hand away from her wrist. "That doesn't mean that I want to see something bad happen to you."

A smirk slid onto my face. "I don't know, Harper. That kind of sounds like you might care." I lifted my hand up, holding my thumb and forefinger apart half an inch. "Even if it's only this much."

Harper dropped her hand away from my face and I instantly felt her absence. She rolled her eyes and crossed her arms over her chest. "You can tell yourself whatever you need to if it will help you sleep better at night."

You would help me sleep better at night.

"I don't know about sleep, but it might help me play better."

She stared at me for a moment before her face cracked. Her eyes crinkled at the sides and her laughter danced across my eardrums. It was the most beautiful thing I had ever heard, and I found myself completely captivated by her. Holding my breath, I smiled and watched her as she shook her head at me.

"You're something else, I'll give you that." She smiled back at me as her laughter dissipated.

I couldn't take my eyes off her and I couldn't stop the words as they rolled off my tongue.

"Go to dinner with me."

Harper's eyes widened. "What?"

Fuck.

My jaw clenched and I wanted to suck the words back in. It was too late. I couldn't take them back now and I had to roll with it.

"I want to take you out to dinner. No strings attached. Just two friends having dinner."

Harper angled her head to the side as she lifted an eyebrow. "Oh. Are we friends now?" Her tone was light and a ghost of a smile played on her lips.

I nodded. "The best of friends."

"Well, in that case, I suppose it would be rude of me to say no." She smiled at me as she shifted her weight on her feet. "Just dinner."

"I just want to feed you. Nothing more." I paused. "Not physically feed you, although I wouldn't be opposed to it."

She stared at me, her eyes dropping to my mouth before meeting my gaze again. "I'm going to pretend you didn't say that and just let you buy me dinner."

Laughter rumbled in my chest and I didn't bother to let myself feel embarrassed. "Get in my car," I told her as I stepped away and made my way to the driver's side. "I know of a place nearby."

"What about my car?"

I glanced over at her from where I was standing, noting the distance between us. "Would you feel better if we drove separately?"

Harper nodded. "Don't want you to get any ideas," she admitted with a wink.

74

"I would never," I scoffed, attempting to feign innocence.

"Yeah, right." She pulled open her door. "You lead the way and I'll follow."

I smiled to myself as I got into my car. I lied when I said I knew of a place nearby. I hadn't thought that far in advance, but I wasn't going to let her down now. Getting her to agree to go to dinner with me was half the battle.

And it was the half I had just won.

Chapter Seven

Harper

I eyed Nico skeptically as we walked to the front doors of the restaurant. When he said that he knew of a place nearby, I wasn't sure what he was talking about. This place wasn't nearly as close as I imagined. I thought he would take us somewhere within a five-minute drive but instead he had me driving closer to twenty minutes from the stadium, in the complete opposite direction of my apartment.

"What is this place?" I asked him as I looked up at the white sign above. All it said was Dare and it gave nothing away from the outside. It was a brick building with blacked out windows and simply had a black door in the front. "Is this even a restaurant?"

It suddenly dawned on me that I really didn't know Nico Cirone. For all I knew, he could be a serial killer, leading me closer to my death.

"Of course it's a restaurant," he said over his shoulder, as he was now a few steps ahead of me. "What else would it possibly be?

He stopped and slowly pulled the door open, stepping to the side for me to walk past him. It was dark inside and I hesitated, pausing my steps as I looked up at him.

"Your secret murder house or something."

Nico raised an eyebrow. "My what?"

I shrugged, still lingering outside the door. "You know, the place where you bring the girls you seduce to kill them."

His face cracked and the sound of his laughter vibrated inside my soul. He flattened his palm over his chest as he momentarily tipped his head back. My mouth grew dry and I swallowed hard, feeling the heat creep across my face. The way he was laughing was doing something to my body that I loved and hated at the same time.

"Jesus, Harper. What kind of a person do you think I am?" He stopped laughing and a smile lingered on his perfect lips as he raised a suspicious eyebrow. "You give me too much credit. I usually just kill them where I find them and dump their body somewhere along the drive home."

Mischief danced in his eyes as I widened mine, attempting to appear shocked.

Nico laughed again and shook his head as he reached out and wrapped his hand around my wrist. "I'm kidding," he said as he pulled me in the direction of the door. "Come on. We're going to be late."

"You made a reservation?" I asked him as I let him pull me into the dark building. My eyes adjusted to the lack of light when I realized there were recessed lights above. They were just dimmed, almost to the point of making the room appear like there weren't any.

Nico nodded and slid his hand down to mine as he released my wrist. His fingers felt foreign as they laced themselves with mine, yet it felt like they belonged there. I wrapped mine around his and held on to him as we stepped through another doorway and entered a hallway.

Soft classical music played through hidden speakers. The hallway was still dimly lit, but it was brighter than the first small room we had entered. There was art decorating all the walls, different abstract paintings without any definitive designs. I turned my head, looking at them as we walked past.

At the end of the hall, there was a small hostess stand and a woman standing behind it. She greeted us with a soft smile and I was finally able to see what the restaurant looked like inside. Outside, the brick gave nothing away. Even up until this point, it was hard to picture what it would look like inside and it wasn't what I was expecting.

It definitely wasn't a secret place for someone to commit murders.

Each booth was tucked into its own little private area, almost like VIP booths with the way they were circular, but each was blocked off with a half wall and there was a small space that you walked through to get to where you sat. The walls were black as well as the furniture. Shimmering chandeliers hung throughout the restaurant and above each booth. It was sleek and minimalistic. Almost futuristic in a way.

"Name?" the woman questioned the two of us.

Nico was still holding my hand. "Cirone."

She scanned an iPad in front of her and tapped on the screen with a pen. "Follow me, please," she instructed as she grabbed two menus and led the way.

Nico followed after her and I fell into step with him until we reached our own little private booth. He let go of my hand, motioning for me to slide in first. I slid around the circular table, situating myself more toward the center of the rounded plush seat. Nico scooted in after me, leaving less than a foot between us as he smiled up at the woman.

"Thank you," he said softly as she handed us the menus.

"Alaina will be your server and should be with you in a moment." She nodded at the two of us before stepping away from the booth and then walked back in the direction she came from.

I glanced around and adjusted in my seat as I looked over at Nico. I took a moment to study his features. His jaw was sharp and his nose was perfectly straight. His cheekbones were high, creating the illusion that his face was a perfectly sculpted masterpiece. I watched as his tongue slid out and he ran it over the cut in his bottom lip.

Holy shit.

My stomach felt warm and I clenched my thighs together. I never thought something like that would turn me on the way it did. I needed to flip the switch off but I couldn't seem to find it. Instead, my breath caught in my throat and I let out a choking sound.

Nico glanced at me with a look of curiosity. "Are you okay?"

Heat crept up my neck and my face was on fire. "I'm fine." I nodded and attempted to clear my throat. "What is this place?"

He set down the menu he was scanning and a soft smile lifted his lips as he folded his hands on the table. "It's cool, right? I've only been here once before, but I love the private setting it offers." He smiled and I watched a dimple form in his left cheek. "The food is really good too."

"It feels like we're the only people here," I told him, my voice quieter than I anticipated. The place had a very intimate ambiance and I couldn't help but wonder who Nico came here with before. A frown pulled my lips downward and I stared down at the menu in front of me as I tried to push the thoughts from my mind. My stomach rolled as I felt uncomfortable sitting here with him.

"What was that?" Nico inquired with curiosity as he scooted closer. "What just happened?"

His presence was consuming me. He was close—too close. I could feel his warmth radiating from his body, encapsulating me. His scent was in my nose, invading my senses. Inhaling deeply, I turned my head to face him just as a college-aged girl stepped up to the half wall by our booth.

"Hi." She smiled as she placed a decanter filled with water on the center of the table. She set down two glasses along with it. "I'm Alaina. Can I get either of you anything to drink? Or maybe an appetizer?"

"I'll take an old fashioned," Nico told her before turning to look at me.

"I'll take a mojito, please."

Nico stared at me and I couldn't quite read the expression on his face.

"Perfect." Alaina grinned. "I'll be right back with your drinks. Would you like to put in an appetizer or anything?"

I glanced at Nico and shook my head. He didn't take his eyes away from mine.

"We're good," he told her, still with his gaze cemented to mine.

Alaina left with the promise of returning soon with our drinks. Nico was still looking at me and I squirmed in my seat, feeling like he was assessing every inch of me with his blue eyes.

"Before she came—what was that?"

I raised an eyebrow, knowing damn well what he was talking about. "It was nothing," I told him, the lie tasting bitter on my tongue.

"Don't lie to me, pretty girl," he mused. "You don't want to find out what happens if you misbehave." He ran his own tongue over the cut on his bottom lip again. "Or maybe you do."

My mouth was instantly dry and I tore my gaze from his as I reached for the decanter. My hand shook as I filled my glass in a haste and swallowed some of the water in a rush.

"Try again, Harper."

I turned back to look at him. "I was wondering who

you came here with before, considering it is such an intimate setting."

His eyes glimmered under the chandelier. "Why is that?"

"Because I would assume it wasn't just a friend."

"Are you jealous, Harper Jensen?" he challenged me.

I glowered at him. "How do you know my last name?"

"I have my ways," he responded with a sly grin. "Now answer my question."

"I'm not jealous," I told him, although my voice sounded far from convincing.

He cocked his head to the side as he positioned his arm across the back of the bench seat. "Then ask me who I came here with."

My heart pounded in my chest and my nostrils flared as he challenged me with his gaze. I didn't want to ask him, but he already had me cornered. A part of me wanted to know. I never once considered the fact that maybe he was seeing someone. I should have turned him down in the parking lot. I shouldn't be here with him.

"Ask me."

I narrowed my eyes at him, feeling the jealousy already seeping into my veins. "Who did you come here with?"

Nico smiled as Alaina returned with our drinks. "My sister, Giana." She disappeared without another word, clearly reading the room, and I was thankful for that.

My face instantly heated and embarrassment swept over me. I looked away from him, but Nico slid his hand under my chin and pulled my face back to look at him. His eyes danced under the lights and he leaned closer, his lips brushing against my ear.

"Don't be embarrassed," he whispered. "I like you jealous."

He slowly pulled away and grabbed his drink. I watched how his lips kissed the rim of the glass and the way his throat bobbed as he swallowed the liquor. I followed suit, taking a sip of mine as I needed the liquid courage. His thigh was now pressed against mine and I wanted him closer.

"Tell me about you, Harper. What makes you smile. What pisses you off."

Alaina returned, thankfully saving me from having to provide Nico with an answer. She took both of our orders, and I had barely even looked over my menu and ordered a pasta dish on the spot as she stood by our booth, patiently waiting. As she walked away, Nico turned his attention back to me.

"Why do you want to know?"

"Because I want to know." His eyes were bright as his smile reached them. "I want to know how to keep that beautiful smile on your lips. I want to know what to avoid so I don't ever piss you off... unless I'm intentionally trying to."

I stared at him for a moment. "I don't know why you've taken such an interest in me. We had one night together—barely, if we're being honest. You could have

84

anyone you want, yet you're chasing after the one you can't have."

"See, that's the thing, love," Nico said slowly, his voice barely audible. "You say I can't have you, but that's where you're wrong. I can have you anywhere I want." His hand was on my thigh. I could feel the warmth of his palm through my leggings. My heart was skipping beats. "I promise no one will ever know. I would never jeopardize your job or anything in your life."

"How can you be so sure?" I breathed as my heart pounded erratically in my chest. "You can't promise that."

He scowled. "You're right, I can't. But I will do everything in my fucking power to make sure no one ever finds out." He paused and I counted three heartbeats before his lips parted again. "Tell me you don't want me, Harper, and I promise I'll leave you alone."

I stared back at him as he trailed his hand farther up my thigh. A heat spread through my veins like wildfire and I swallowed roughly. "I don't want you," I whispered, my voice sticking like there was peanut butter in my throat.

His lips twitched. "If you're going to lie to me, love, at least make it believable." His tongue slid out as he wet his lips. He slid his hands between my thighs, his fingers brushed against my pussy. I inhaled sharply as the friction sent a bolt of lightning through my body. "I'll give you one more try to convince me that you don't want me."

A shiver slid down my spine and he slowly circled

his thumb around my clit. Even through two layers of clothing, he had no problem finding it. I shifted under his touch, wanting to get away from him because I didn't want him to have that satisfaction, yet I wanted to get even closer. "I don't want you, Nico," I choked out.

He pulled his bottom lip between his teeth and my eyes dropped down to his mouth. I watched as he left crescent-shaped marks in his flesh. He continued to work his thumb against me and I didn't try to stop him. I didn't want him to stop. My body was on fire, simultaneously tingling and there was something building deep inside me.

"You're a terrible liar, Harper," Nico growled as he released his lip and pulled his hand away from me. I instantly felt his absence and my clit was throbbing, still needing him and the release he was pushing me closer to.

My eyebrows scrunched together and my eyes sliced back to his. "Why did you stop?" I breathed.

He smirked as he used the same hand he just had between my thighs to lift his drink to his lips. I watched the way his throat elongated as he took a long swallow of the liquor. Nico set the glass back on the table in front of him.

"I don't reward liars."

My breath caught in my throat as I tore my gaze from his and stared at the table in front of me. Something about his tone, the way the words spilled from his lips—I couldn't help myself but feel a deep-seated need inside.

Maybe it was because he left me hanging. There was unfinished business between us and he suddenly tipped the tables on me. He left things even more intense than they were before. There was a part of me that wanted to believe him. He said that no one would find out. He gave me no reason to not trust him.

I let out the breath I was holding as I directed my gaze back to his.

"What do I have to do for you to reward me?"

His lips curled upward. "Tell me the truth or convince me otherwise."

My stomach fluttered and I traced the indents in his lip before looking back into his eyes.

"I want you, Nico."

Aliana suddenly appeared as she stepped over to our table with our plates of food.

Nico whipped his head in her direction. "We'll actually be taking these to go and I will take the check."

"Very well," she nodded before taking our food away to box it up without another word.

Nico directed his gaze back to me. "I'm taking you home with me so I can reward you properly without any fucking distractions." He paused for a beat, his eyes searching mine. "If you don't want me to do that, now would be the time to say something."

I swallowed hard and my heart beat against my rib cage.

I should have told him no, but I didn't.

"That's exactly what I want you to do."

Chapter Eight

Nico

Harper insisted on driving her car to my apartment, even though I had tried to convince her to ride with me. She didn't want to leave it far away, which I could understand. That didn't dismiss the intense need to have her right beside me right now.

I whipped my car into the parking garage underneath my building and Harper followed behind me. I lost sight of her momentarily as she turned and went over to where the guest parking was. My spot wasn't too far so I slid the car into it and put it in park, before killing the engine. Grabbing the food from my passenger seat, I climbed out and headed in the direction of where Harper was.

As I pressed the lock button on my key fob, the beeping sound echoed throughout the garage. When I rounded a row of cars, I spotted Harper walking through the garage looking for me. My footsteps were light and quiet as I moved closer to her. She must have spotted me from the corner of her eye, as she whipped her head to the side and her face relaxed when she saw me.

"Hey," she said as I stopped in front of her. Her cheeks were tinted pink and her eyes were bright. She nervously shifted her weight on her feet, but there was no indication that she didn't want to be here right now.

"Come with me," I told her, holding my hand out for her as I held on to our bag of food with the other hand. "Let's get inside and eat before the food gets too cold."

Harper slid her palm against mine without hesitation and her fingers laced with mine. I looked at her once more and she smiled back at me. "Good, because I'm starving."

So am I... but not for food.

I led her into the building and we stepped onto the elevator. After punching in my code, it took us straight to my floor. As the doors slid open, Harper looked at me with an eyebrow raised. "This is your place?"

I nodded and pulled her inside my condo before the elevator doors slid shut. The walls were painted a darker gray and it had a clean, slate like aesthetic. My mother and sister were the two who decorated my place after I picked out the color scheme. There was a masculine feel to it, yet it was modern and industrial.

"It's really nice," Harper said softly as she followed me into the kitchen area. It had an open floor plan concept with the kitchen, dining, and living room area.

I set the bag of food down on the island and turned around before pulling Harper to me. She exhaled softly as the front of her body collided with mine. Sliding my hand along the side of her jaw, I lifted her chin so she was looking up at me.

"I'm starving," I growled as I dragged my thumb along her plump bottom lip. "I'm ready to eat now."

Harper's eyes searched mine as she slid her hands around the back of my neck. "The food is right behind you."

A smirk pulled on my lips and I shook my head. "Not what I'm hungry for, love," I told her as my face dipped down to hers as my hands dropped to her waist. "I'm hungry for you."

My mouth crashed into hers and Harper didn't miss a beat. Her hands were running through the hair at the nape of my neck and she was wrapping her legs around my waist as I lifted her into the air. She was in my arms, her tongue was in my mouth, and I set her down on the counter as I deepened the kiss. Our tongues danced together and my lips bruised hers, but I wasn't holding back.

She was mine for the taking and I was going to take every fucking thing she was willing to give me.

Harper's legs were still around my waist and my cock was hard, pressing against her through the material of our clothing. She rolled her hips, grinding herself against me as I slid my hands along her thighs. Our tongues danced together and I breathed her in. I kissed her until we were both breathless, but it wasn't enough. I wanted more.

I wanted it all.

Pulling away from her, I trailed my lips along her

jaw before traveling down the length of her neck. Her moans slid along my eardrums like silk and my hands slid under her ass as I continued to move down her body. She released her legs from my waist and I was still standing between her legs as I looked at her.

Reaching for the bottom hem of her shirt, I began to push it up her torso. Harper's eyes were hooded, her gaze heated, and her chest rose and fell with every ragged breath she took. I slowly pushed it up until she was lifting her arms into the air. I pulled it away from her and tossed it onto the floor.

Harper leaned back slightly, planting her hands on the countertop as I inched closer to her. My mouth found the tender skin in the crook of her neck and I made my way along her collarbone while reaching around her back to undo the clasp of her bra. Within a fraction of a second, I removed it from her body and threw it wherever her shirt went.

My mouth traveled down to her breasts and they fit perfectly in my hands. Her skin was soft and I pulled one nipple in between my lips as I rolled the other between my thumb and forefinger. Her chest rose and fell faster and my cock strained against my pants.

Switching breasts, I continued my assault on her flesh before I began to slowly bend my knees and trail my lips down her torso. Harper's hands were in my hair and she was pulling my head up to look at her.

"What are you doing?" she breathed, her eyes frantically searching mine.

I tilted my head to the side as I slid my hands under

her ass and grasped the waistband of her leggings. "I told you that I was hungry."

Her eyes widened slightly as her mouth formed in the shape of an *O*.

The corners of my lips lifted. "Be a good girl and lay back for me so I can eat."

I began to pull her leggings down, pulling her panties with them. Harper didn't utter another word, lifting her hips instead as I peeled her clothes from her body until she was completely naked lying on my kitchen counter.

Standing between her legs, I allowed myself the pleasure of taking a mental picture of her. I wanted this moment cemented in my mind for the rest of eternity. "So fucking perfect," I murmured as I pressed the tips of my fingers between her breasts and trailed them down her body. "I could stare at you like this for the rest of my fucking life. Spread out and ready for me to take what is mine."

"Yours?" she lifted an eyebrow as she stared up at me.

"I'm going to ruin you for anyone else, love," I breathed, a smirk pulling on my lips as I lowered myself to my knees between her legs. Sliding my hands under her ass, I pulled her hips to the very edge of the counter so her pussy was directly in my face. "So, yes. That makes every inch of you mine."

As I ran my tongue against her, Harper inhaled sharply, instantly sliding her hands through my hair. Her nails dug into my scalp as I moved my mouth against her. My eyelids fell shut and I circled my tongue around her clit, just barely brushing it with each movement. Harper hooked her thighs over my shoulders and I smiled against her pussy as she lifted her hips in the air.

Pulling back, I slapped her pussy with my palm. Her body jolted, her head lifting up in a rush as she let out a yelp. She was breathless, her cheeks tinted pink as her wide eyes met mine.

"What was that for?"

I gripped her ass in my hands tighter. "Don't be greedy, love. I promise I'll let you come—but only when I'm ready to."

Her eyebrows pulled together and she pouted. "That's not fair."

"It actually is. All you have to do is exactly what I say and you'll be rewarded."

"I haven't disobeyed you," she argued with a heated look in her eyes. Her breathing was ragged and shallow. "I've been good."

"I'll be the judge of that."

I silenced her with my mouth as I pulled her clit between my lips and sucked on it hard. Harper let out another moan and her hands were still in my hair. I continued my assault on the most sensitive part of her body, working my mouth and tongue around her clit. I wasn't ready for her to come yet, but I wanted her close. Right there at the edge where she could almost reach out and grab it yet just out of her grasp.

Harper was a mess of breathless moans, her hips involuntarily bucking as I continued to focus solely on her clit. Her body began to grow tense. My balls were constricting, drawing closer to my body. She was getting closer and her thighs were beginning to clamp around my head just as I pulled my mouth away from her pussy again.

She let out a frustrated groan and I looked up at her, her pussy wet and glistening in my face. "Don't stop, Nico," she moaned, trying to push my mouth back to her. "I'm so close."

I shook my head. "Beg for it."

"I don't beg for anything."

My mouth twitched and I slapped her pussy again, earning another yelp from her. "For me, you do."

She let out a breath. "Please, Nico."

Slap. My hand came down on her pussy again.

"I don't believe that you actually want it."

Harper let out a low moan and her eyes practically rolled back in her head. "I do. God, I do."

Slap.

"Not your god, love. He can only take you to heaven. Where I'm taking you is a place he could never take you."

"Please, Nico. I want it," she said breathlessly. "I want you to fuck me with your mouth. Please let me come."

Slap.

"Almost, love."

"I'll do whatever you want if you let me come," she pleaded, her voice an octave higher. "I'm yours. All of me. Please let me come. I need it more than anything."

A smile pulled on my lips and I dove back in. My tongue was relentless and I rolled it over her clit again and again. Harper was a mess of moans, her hands were gripping my hair, and her hips began to buck again.

Gripping her ass, I held her down and fucked her with my mouth until she was falling over the edge, coming all over my tongue. She cried out, her sounds consuming me as her body erupted from her orgasm. It tore through her body with such an intensity, she was shattering into a million pieces on my counter.

I didn't stop until she was shaking from pleasure and her legs fell away from the sides of my head. Lifting my head, I slowly eased myself back to my feet as I stood at the edge of the counter. Harper's eyes were glazed over, her breathing was erratic, and there was nothing but pleasure washing through her bright irises.

"Are you ready to take my cock like a good fucking girl?"

She gave me a lazy smile as she pushed herself back up onto her elbows. "That depends on whether or not you're ready to fuck me like I deserve to be fucked."

I couldn't help but smile down at her. "Maybe I'll shove my cock down your throat instead. Teach you a lesson about that damn attitude of yours."

"You sure it's big enough to even make it to the back of my throat?"

She was really fucking testing me and my cock was as hard as a goddamn rock. I liked her sass and her attitude, but I also wanted to fuck it out of her.

Grabbing her hips, I flipped her over onto her stomach in one fluid movement. She yelped in surprise and I pushed my pants and underwear down to my ankles before pulling her so she was folded over the edge of the counter.

As I pressed the tip of my cock to her pussy, I hesitated. "I need to grab a condom."

Harper looked back at me and shook her head. "I'm on the pill." She paused for a beat, need glimmering in her eyes. "Fuck me raw."

Goddamn.

I slammed into her without another word, filling her to the hilt as she cried out. Leaning forward, I pressed my lips to her ears. "Still think that it's not big enough?"

"Size doesn't really matter. It's whether or not you know how to use it."

Standing back upright, I slowly pulled my cock out until just the tip was left inside her. "Let me ruin you, love," I murmured as I slammed back into her.

"Do your worst."

Chapter Nine

Harper

Nico's fingertips dug into my skin as he grasped my hips and pounded into me over and over again. Each thrust had him filling me completely, filling my body with a pleasure I had never experienced before. I'd never been one to have an orgasm just from someone being inside me, but Nico was pushing me closer to the edge of ecstasy and I couldn't think straight at this point.

"Fuck, you were made to take my cock, Harper," Nico groaned from behind me. His one hand was now planted against the small of my back, holding me firmly in place. The other was still gripping my hip with such force, I knew there would be marks left behind.

And I didn't even care.

I wanted his marks all over my skin. I tried to resist him as long as I could, but I was proving that I wasn't strong enough to ignore his charm. Now that he had me bent over his counter, I was going to take advantage of every second with him. Every feeling. Every moment.

Even if it were fleeting—because it had to be. There could never be anything more than this between us, and it fit both of our agendas.

But when he went and said things like that, I didn't like the way my heart did a little flutter. It added in an extra beat and I hated it.

The edge of the countertop was digging into my flesh as Nico continued to fuck me harder with each thrust. He was fucking me relentlessly, with no mercy—and I wanted more.

"Don't stop," I moaned.

"Don't plan on it, love," he growled as he dropped his lips back to my ear. He was surrounding me, consuming me, with his chest pressed against my back. "I'm going to fuck you until you split in two."

I turned my head to the side, my cheek pressed against the cool granite surface. "You're going to have to fuck me harder to do that."

Nico looked at me and I stared at him from the corner of my eye. "You like challenging me, don't you? Why don't you tell me what you want instead?"

"I told you to do your worst, Nico. So do it."

He shook his head. "Not yet. I'm going to fuck you now until we both come, but it will be nowhere close to doing my worst. That will come later. I have every intention of fucking you until you can't think straight, but for now I've changed my mind. I'm greedy and I'm taking what I want right now instead."

I tried to glare at him and Nico ran his hand down the side of my neck before pulling away. He slowly eased out of me, only to slam back into me again. There was nothing gentle about the way he was moving against me, and I wanted it all. Every inch of pain and pleasure mixed together until we couldn't tell one from the other.

He was pushing me closer and closer to the edge. My eyes were rolling back in my head from the ecstasy racing through my veins. My legs felt like they were going to give out as a warmth spread from the pit of my stomach and throughout the rest of my body.

"I feel you, Harper," Nico moaned as he moved both hands to hold on to my waist. "Come for me, love. Come all over my cock while I fill you with my cum."

His words as he thrust into me were enough to send me over the edge, free falling into the abyss. My orgasm tore through my body like a whirlwind and I was clenching around him as it felt like I was floating into the air. The heat that spread through me felt like a wildfire that could never be tamed. My eyes clamped shut and I yelled out his name as I did exactly as he told me.

"Fuck," he growled as his grip tightened around my waist. He slammed into me once more and I felt the warmth of him as he lost himself inside me. We were both a mix of moans and heavy breathing and it felt like him holding me was the only thing that was keeping me from floating through the ceiling.

That wasn't even his worst. I couldn't even begin to imagine what that must feel like compared to this.

Nico slowly eased out of me and pressed his lips to the center of my back. My legs shook and felt like they were going to give out. I instantly felt his absence, but suddenly he pulled me away from the counter as he lifted me into his arms.

"What are you doing?" I questioned him as I rolled my head to look at him.

Nico gave me a lazy smile. "Taking you to my bed to clean you up and get you comfortable."

His words warmed my soul and I was taken by surprise with his attentiveness. I didn't question him as he laid me down on his plush mattress that had all-black bedding. I didn't say a word as I watched him disappear into the bathroom, nor did I when he came back with a warm washcloth.

"I need my clothes."

Nico chuckled lightly and shook his head. "I promise you, you don't."

I should have felt uncomfortable, still completely naked under his gaze, but there was something about him that just felt right. He felt familiar, even though I didn't really know him that well. He made me feel safe and I let him tuck me under the covers of his bed as he rose to his feet.

"Make yourself comfortable," he told me as he handed me the remote. "I'm going to go heat up our food and we can have dinner in bed."

Hesitantly, I took the remote from him and eyed him skeptically. "Do you always walk around your house naked and expect your guests to do the same?"

Nico laughed again and shook his head. "Only with you, love."

He left the room without another word and I sat up straight, my back pressing against the pillows while pulling the blankets up to cover my exposed chest. I turned on the TV and flipped through Netflix before settling on a true crime docuseries when he finally returned with our food.

Nico had heated everything up on separate plates and was balancing them in his hands as he walked back into the room. He handed me mine before setting his on the nightstand. I watched him walk back out of the room, but he was only gone for half a minute before he came back in with two glasses and a bottle of wine.

He popped the cork and filled both of our glasses before climbing under the sheets. We both sat in silence, eating our food and sipping our wine as we learned about the case they were trying to solve.

"Do you watch a lot of stuff like this?" he asked while lifting his glass to take a sip of his wine.

I swallowed a mouthful of pasta and nodded. "Yeah. I like true crime type stuff."

"That makes sense with what you said at Dare, thinking I was going to take you to some secret location to murder you."

Laughter spilled from my lips. "Hey, it's always the ones who are charming and attractive that you have to be careful with."

Nico stared at me for a moment and I looked over at him as mischief danced in his blue irises. He didn't say a word, but simply smiled at me before diverting his gaze back to the TV as he continued to eat. We finished the rest of our meal in silence and the air between us was sparked with electricity. It was palpable and I was afraid if I touched him, I would certainly be electrocuted.

After we were done, Nico took both of our plates and stacked them on his nightstand before filling up our glasses again. The red wine splashed against the clear cup and I allowed my eyes a moment to truly appreciate his body. The blankets stopped just below his belly button and my gaze traveled across the planes of his muscular form.

"So, Harper," Nico started as he shifted in the bed to face me. He had his elbow propped on the pillow and was resting his hand on his head. "What made you move to Orchid Beach?"

His question caught me off guard and I took a long sip of my wine. "I needed a change of scenery and had just gotten out of a relationship. I went to Boston for college and ended up staying there after I graduated. It just never really felt like home, so I decided I'd move somewhere that I could make my own home."

"Where are you originally from?"

I was surprised he didn't question me on my relationship.

"I was born and raised in Denver. I considered moving back there, but I left Denver because I wanted more than just mountains," I told him. As much as I loved Colorado, I wanted to see and experience other places in the country or the world. I didn't want to live there for my entire life. "What about you? Where is home for you?"

"I actually grew up here," he said simply with a shrug. "My family lives across the state now, though, so

I do miss them. They come and visit occasionally and I try to go back home to see them when I can."

"That must be nice." I smiled at him as I adjusted myself on the bed to lay the same way he was, although I made sure to keep my chest covered. "Are you all close?"

A wave of pain washed through his irises as he looked past me and nodded. "My family has always been extremely supportive of what I do. After my mother passed away, we were all a little lost, but in time, it has made us closer than ever."

I stared at him for a moment, my heart clenching in my chest while simultaneously breaking for him. He was still hurting, his wounds were still open, and it was clearly written all over his face. I wanted to wrap my arms around him and tell him it would all be okay, but those were just words. They changed nothing. They would never erase the hole in his heart from losing his mother.

"I am so sorry, Nico," I said softly as I continued to watch him. "I know that doesn't really help, but I really am sorry for your loss. I can't even imagine how that must feel for you."

He slowly pulled his gaze back to mine and gave me a sad smile. "Thanks, love. It's been two years already, but sometimes it feels like we just lost her yesterday. I appreciate your kindness, though."

"If you ever want to talk about anything, I am always here for you."

"Actually, I do want to talk about something." His smile grew tighter and he raised an eyebrow. "You just got out of a relationship before moving here? What happened?"

Shit.

My stomach instantly sank and I swallowed roughly. "I was dating someone I had met in college but I realized he wasn't the one."

"How did you know that?" he asked without missing a beat.

"Because he gave me an ultimatum. I was in the middle of building my own portfolio and trying to find a professional job. He wanted me to give everything up and follow him." I paused for a moment, shaking my head. I didn't miss Connor at all, but I hated what he did to me. "I had to choose. Either follow him or he was moving on without me. I didn't follow him."

Nico stared at me for a moment and slowly sat up in bed. He took my glass of wine and set it on his night-stand along with his own glass. As he turned back to face me, he closed the distance between us. His fingers were soft as he brushed a stray hair from my face while sliding the other around my back and under the covers.

He pulled me flush against him, his blue eyes shining down at me as he rolled me onto my back. A smile lifted the corners of his lips as he settled between my legs.

"I'm glad you didn't follow him."

I smiled back at him just as his face dipped down to mine.

So was I.

Chapter Ten

Nico

As I rolled over in bed, I slid my hand over the sheet feeling for her. My eyebrows pulled together and I peeled my eyelids open as I noticed that the bed was empty. It was still warm where she was laying and I moved over, burying my face in the pillow. It still smelled like her and I inhaled deeply, savoring her scent.

The bathroom door opened and she stepped into my room, fully clothed. She didn't notice me at first and her footsteps were quiet as she moved about the room, collecting the rest of her things. I watched her in silence with one eye as the other was pressed against the pillow.

She glanced over at me once more and I kept my breathing steady with my eye barely open. Her gaze lingered but she didn't take a step closer. Instead, she turned on her heel and was as quiet as a mouse as she made her way to my bedroom door.

"Leaving without saying goodbye?" I quipped as I lifted my head to look at her.

Harper gasped and turned around to face me. "I didn't know you were awake."

"So, you were still going to leave anyways?" I threw back. "You surprise me, Harper Jensen. You didn't strike me as a hit-it-and-quit-it type of girl."

She stared at me as she defensively crossed her arms over her chest. "That's not how I am at all. You were peaceful and I didn't want to disrupt you."

"I call bullshit," I argued as I sat up in bed. "You thought I was still asleep and saw it as your chance to escape. Are you trying to run away from me, love?"

She laughed softly and the sound was like a melody. "You're ridiculous. I'm going home, Nico. I need to get a shower and have shit I need to do."

"Shower here."

Harper shook her head and waved her hand. "Bye, Nico."

"Text me so I know you got home all right."

She was already walking through my apartment. "I'll think about it," she called out as I heard the elevator ding. She was in it and the doors were sliding closed before she gave me a chance to respond.

Rolling over in bed, I grabbed my phone and opened up our message thread and began typing.

NICO

> If I don't hear from you, I will come and make sure you're okay myself.

It didn't take long for her to respond. She wasn't

even out of my building yet.

HARPER

You don't even know where I live.

A smile pulled on my lips.

NICO

Don't underestimate me, love. I can
easily find that out if I need to.

I didn't need to see a response back from her. I only
needed one from when she got home. Locking the
screen of my phone, I set it down on my bed and
headed into my bathroom to brush my teeth and relieve
myself. I had to get to practice in a few hours, so I
quickly hopped in the shower, even though I would be
getting back in later on.

It didn't take me long to wash my body and hair. As
I stepped out of the shower and toweled off, I heard my
phone ringing from my bedroom. My stomach did a
somersault and I wanted to punch myself in the nuts for
a reality check.

There was no reason for me to be acting like a little
boy who had his first crush. Harper wasn't the first girl
that I was ever with and given the circumstances, I'm
sure she wouldn't be the last. Although, I wouldn't
complain if she were the only girl I would ever be with
again. She does something to me—something I need to
shut off.

We agreed that this was as far as this would ever go.
Especially when so much was at stake for Harper. My

feelings would only complicate things more and I needed to bury them down, deep.

It was in moments like this I wish I had my mom.

When I walked back into my room, I saw three unread messages. Two were from Wes and one was from Harper. I opened hers first.

HARPER

I'm home safe and taking a much-needed nap before I run my errands. Thanks again for last night ;)

I smiled to myself.

NICO

Anytime, love. Text me later.

I closed out of our messages and ignored Wes's as I went through my contacts. I found my sister's name and tapped on it to FaceTime her. When our mom died, there were moments that it felt like it was just the two of us. Our father was still present, but he wasn't really there. A part of him died that day too. And Giana and I realized we really had to stick together.

"Hey, Nic," she signed to me as she answered the call. Her bright blue eyes that matched mine shined back at me and she flashed her white teeth with her grin. We both favored our mother.

"What are you doing?" I signed back to her as I dropped down onto my bed.

G gave me a look of suspicion. *"What are you doing? You never call me this early. What's wrong?"*

"I just wanted to talk to you. Feeling a little alone and

shit."

Giana frowned, but gave me a knowing look. *"Missing Mom?"*

I nodded. *"And you, obviously."*

"Well, duh," she signed as she let out the softest laugh. *"I would miss me too."*

Giana lost her hearing when she was a child. She got really sick and ended up spending a chunk of time in the hospital with heart issues. The medications they had her on caused permanent hearing loss and even though she could still physically talk, she mainly only signed now.

"What's up, though, Nico?" Her expression was filled with concern. *"Did you get into some kind of trouble?"*

I shook my head. *"No, I'm not in trouble. I don't know. My head is all over the place and I'm not thinking straight."*

Giana's eyebrows pulled together. *"Stop being cryptic and spit it out."*

"I met this girl," I signed to her. I had talked to my sister about girls before but that was back in high school. It wasn't a normal thing for me to bring someone up like this to her.

Her face lit up. *"Tell me more."*

"She works for the team as a photographer. She's off-limits, but I can't get her out of my fucking head, G."

My sister's eyes widened. *"Don't tell me... you've already gotten involved with her, haven't you?"*

"It's complicated," I signed back to her as a sigh escaped me. *"It's honestly nothing. We're both just having fun."*

"At what expense?" She gave me with a look of disap-

proval. "*You've worked too hard to get this far to just simply throw it away in such a careless manner.*"

I narrowed my eyes at my sister. "*My career is safe. Sure, it wouldn't look good, but it would be fine.*"

Giana rolled her eyes and shook her head. "*Of course. The star athlete always comes out of a scandal unscathed.*"

"*Whoa,*" I signed back at her as her words felt like a knife twisting in my gut. "*You're supposed to be on my side, remember?*"

"*I am on your side, but I don't want you to get into any trouble and I don't want you to ruin some girl's life because you can't seem to keep your dick in your pants.*"

"*That's the thing,*" I told her as my eyes bounced back and forth between hers. "*I don't want to ruin her life, but I can't leave her alone, G. She's different.*"

Giana pursed her lips. "*Is there any way that you can continue to see her and not ruin her life?*"

I shrugged. "*I'm trying to figure that out.*" I paused for a moment and frowned. "*I didn't call you to be lectured. I called you because I was missing Mom and you're the closest thing I have to her. All she ever wanted was the two of us to be happy in life.*"

My sister's face fell and sadness washed through her expression. "*I want you to be happy too, Nic. I just want you to be rational and careful.*"

"*I always am.*"

Giana didn't look convinced but she didn't push any further. "*This girl—she must be special if she has your attention. I can't remember the last time you talked to me about being interested in someone.*"

"That's what freaks me out the most," I explained to her as my heart picked up the pace in my chest. *"I should be able to just let it go, but I can't. I don't want to stop seeing her. I want to be around her any chance I get."*

G's chest rose and fell as she let out a sigh. *"If you like her that much, try not to fuck it up. Mom wouldn't want you fucking up someone else's life because of your stupidity."*

My sister had a point, yet I couldn't seem to see past Harper and wanting her. It was as if I had blinders on. I knew that there were risks to seeing her, yet I didn't care. Harper had her reservations and I was respectful of that. She was beginning to seem like she wasn't too concerned with the consequences either.

Giana snapped her fingers at me, as she could tell I wasn't paying attention. I gave her a sympathetic smile and focused back on her hands as she signed to me once again.

"I know this is a big ask, but can you just have a conversation with her? Make sure the two of you are on the same page before proceeding."

I nodded. *"I will. I promise."*

Wes's name flashed across my screen and I let out a breath of relief that my sister missed.

"I hate to run, but Wes is calling and we have practice in two hours so I should see what he wants."

Giana laughed and rolled her eyes. *"Heaven forbid that Weston Cole should ever have to wait to talk to you."*

I laughed along with her and shrugged. *"He's one of those people who refuses to be ignored."*

My sister smiled at me. *"Sounds awfully familiar."*

"Bye, G. I love you and thank you," I signed to her with

a smile. I didn't really have any expectations for having a conversation with her, but I just wanted to talk to her. Kind of like the same way I would have talked to my mother if she were still alive.

A part of me regretted telling my sister because I knew she wasn't going to let this go now. She would probably text me later in the week to bother me about whether or not I talked to Harper and what she said in response. G would never accept breadcrumbs. She needed the whole damn loaf of bread.

"Love you, Nic. Don't be a fucking idiot."

She ended the call and I tapped on Wes's name to call him back since he got sent to voicemail. He picked up on the third ring, almost as if he were making me wait before he picked it up.

"What are you doing?" he asked me, getting straight to the point. "Are you busy?"

"Nah," I told him as I got up from my bed. "Come on over."

"Sweet. I'll be there in ten minutes."

Wes ended the call and I sighed. I didn't feel like entertaining him, but he was also really good at entertaining himself. This was typical of him and sometimes I wondered if he just didn't enjoy his own company. He was my best friend, though, so who was I to tell him no?

Plus, maybe he and his bullshit would distract me from my own thoughts.

I needed to get Harper out of my mind.

And I was beginning to question whether or not that was even possible.

Chapter Eleven

Harper

I had successfully been managing to avoid any run-ins with Nico after leaving his apartment the other morning. Phillip switched up our assignments so I only saw Nico while he was playing. We'd been talking, but I had been able to avoid hanging out with him, even though he had asked a few times.

The other night scared me. The way he was with me —the way he made me feel. I never had an experience with anyone else like I did with him, and it confused the hell out of me. I shouldn't have been involving myself with him in the first place. Not with my job at stake. Yet I couldn't help myself.

And it was really hard turning him down every time he tried to see me this week.

I knew there needed to be some distance between us. I couldn't let myself get involved with him on a personal level and I felt like we were already toeing that line. If we kept things superficial and at face value, there was no reason to go forming any attachments.

Phillip assigned me at the players' entrance again and I couldn't help but feel a mixture of excitement and dread. There was no way of avoiding Nico if I saw him while walking in. I tried to get Ava to switch with me, but she told me it wasn't allowed. Once we had our assignments, they were ours. Do or die, I had to get the shots, and unfortunately for me, I had gotten some that the organization really liked.

It was a true compliment but I didn't want to come face to face with Nico. He had kept things pleasant when we talked through texts the past few days, but seeing him in person was a completely different story. He had a way of drawing things out of me. And I had a feeling he wasn't going to let me go until he got what he wanted… whatever that might be this time.

My phone vibrated as an email came through and I quickly checked it as I had a few minutes before anyone would be walking in. It was someone Ava put me in contact with that was looking for a wedding photographer. They were highly impressed with my work and wanted to hire me. A smile pulled on my lips as I sent them a quick response back with the promise of connecting and going over details next week.

As the guys came rolling in, I was already sitting on the floor with my camera in position. I got a few of the guys laughing and talking as they walked together. Some were very serious, some had headphones or earbuds in and were working on their mental game. It was an experience in itself, just getting to witness their own habits as they got prepared to go out on the ice.

In typical fashion, Nico and Wes came walking in

and were toward the back of the pack. They were never late, but they were always one of the last ones here. Wes had another wrinkled outfit on and I couldn't help but stifle a laugh as I took a few shots of the two of them. Wes was talking on the phone this time and Nico already had his eyes on me.

I wanted the floor to open up and swallow me whole so I could avoid his piercing blue eyes. He stopped in front of me and Wes nodded as he walked past. He didn't glance back at Nico, which was unusual. The two of them were stuck together like glue. Nico's eyes were on mine and he waited until the door closed behind the guys before parting his perfect lips.

Lips I'd already touched and tasted.

My mouth went dry and my tongue darted out in an attempt to wet my own lips. Nico's gaze dropped down to my mouth, lingering for a moment. I watched his throat move as he swallowed and he slid his hands into the front pockets of his suit jacket before bringing his eyes back to mine.

"You've been avoiding me, love," he said, his voice low yet soft. "I think I have an idea why, but I want to hear it from you."

I slowly set my camera down in my bag and rose to my feet to face him head-on. "You could have asked me this before today. You knew that if you had me cornered here, there was no way I could avoid answering you."

Nico stood perfectly still and simply smiled. He didn't need to answer me as we both knew it was the truth. He wasn't an erratic, uncalculated person. Everything he did was thought out and planned. I didn't know if I would want to see what an unhinged Nico Cirone looked like. I saw him on the ice in fights, but even those looked like he had run through a game plan in his own mind of how he was going to conduct himself.

He was always controlled and never out of line.

"Tell me why, Harper."

I stared back at him for a moment. "If you already think you know the reason, then there's no reason for me to say it."

"I need you to confirm it. That way I can chase away your fears."

His words spread a warmth through my body and my heart did that stupid little thing it did when he was around. "I can't get attached to you, Nico. I need things simple with no strings. I just got out of a bad relationship a few months ago and I'm not looking for a rebound."

"I would never be your rebound, love," he said as his eyes stared directly into mine. "There wouldn't be anyone after me."

My heart did that damn thing again and skipped at least four beats in my chest. I couldn't let myself feel anything with him and I needed him to give me the same in return.

"It wouldn't ever work, Nico. You know we can never be anything." I paused for a moment, watching a shadow pass over his expression. "We're friends, but nothing more. We might do things we probably shouldn't, but that's all it can ever be. You already know the risks we are running by doing that."

Nico was silent as he stared at me with ice sliding over his eyes. "You're right. We're nothing."

"That's not what I meant," I told him in a rush, instantly regretting saying anything. It was clear I had offended him or hurt his feelings. I shouldn't care. I didn't want these feelings and I didn't think he did either.

He shook his head and gave me nothing with his blank expression. "I know exactly what you mean, Harper."

I didn't think he really did. Hell, I didn't even know what I really meant or what I wanted. He was already clouding my brain and I needed the fog to be lifted so I could see clearly.

"I'm not going to ruin your career or fuck up your life because I enjoy spending time with you. Being inside you was just an added benefit." He paused for a moment, his chest rising as he inhaled deeply. "You made yourself crystal clear. If you decide to change your mind, you know where to find me."

He went to walk past me, but my hand instinctively darted out to grab him. "Nico, wait." I pulled him back and he turned to face me. His eyes slowly searched mine. "I don't want whatever this is between us to be done."

His eyes stopped moving as he focused in on my gaze and took a step closer to me. "Then what do you want, Harper? You're giving me fucking whiplash with your mixed signals. One night you're in my bed, the next you're giving me short responses and then telling me we can never be anything more than friends."

"You know I can't afford to lose my job."

He slid his hand to cup the side of my face as he ran his thumb across my bottom lip. "Fuck your job. Come live with me and let me take care of you."

"Absolutely not. I won't be some kept woman—ever. I need to have my own thing too." His face was inching closer to mine and my heart was pounding erratically in my chest. "What are you doing, Nico? Someone might see us."

Nico looked around us and was suddenly backing me up until we were stepping through a curtain that blocked off an area that had workout equipment. Some of the players used it for conditioning, or if they were recovering from an injury, they worked out down here during the game. There was no one in the area right now and Nico walked me backward until my back was pressed against the concrete wall.

"Is that better, love? No one will see us here."

"Someone could walk in at any time," I countered.

Nico chuckled softly and pressed his finger to my lips. "Shh. You don't want anyone to hear us, do you? They'd definitely find out about us then."

I swallowed roughly as he dragged his finger down both of my lips. His eyes searched mine once before his mouth was crashing into mine. I leaned my head back and he ran his hand down to my throat as he lightly wrapped his hand around it. He had me pressed against the wall and his cock was hard against my stomach.

He inhaled me, draining the oxygen from my lungs as he kissed me with an urgent need. His tongue traced the seam of my lips and I parted them as he entered my mouth. Our tongues were tangled together and my head was swimming from the ecstasy of him kissing me. His hand was still around my throat and mine were around the back of his neck, pulling him closer.

Anyone could have walked in and I didn't even think I would have fully cared. Fuck my job. Fuck it all. Nico Cirone had me under his spell and there was no way I was getting out of it now. Like a spider with a web, he already had me tangled up in him and he was ready to devour me.

He abruptly pulled away, leaving me completely breathless. His eyes were back on my mouth and he ran his thumb along my bottom lip. "I'm going to end up fucking you against this wall if we don't stop now."

"Then don't stop," I told him even though my brain was screaming at me for being a fucking idiot. His eyes jumped to mine and I knew he wasn't joking.

"Don't want you to lose your job," he said with a bite in his tone. I felt his absence the moment he stepped away from me and a shiver slid down my spine. I wanted him to come back to me, but instead he was turning around and walking the other way.

"Where are you going?" I asked him, my voice barely audible as I stayed in place where he left me against the wall.

He glanced at me over his shoulder. "I've got a game to play, love." He smirked with a wink. "We can pick up where we left off later."

"I'm supposed to go out with Ava after the game."

Nico lingered for a moment with mischief dancing in his eyes. "Don't worry, love. I'll find you."

Without another word, he turned back around and pushed through the curtain. I was frozen against the wall. My heart felt like it was going to beat out of my chest and I was still struggling to catch my breath. I had no idea where any of this was going with him, but I was willing to roll the dice and see where we would end up.

He was about to turn my entire life upside down.

I just didn't know it yet...

Chapter Twelve

Nico

As we all filed down the tunnel back to the locker room, the guys were exhausted but still hyped from our win. I couldn't help but smile as I thought about Harper and our encounter before the game. Perhaps that was something I needed to make more of a habit because I ended up with seven points during the entire game tonight.

She was definitely a good luck charm for sure.

Sitting down on the bench, I began to strip out of my gear and was careful to save my ball of tape. As I slid it into my bag, my phone vibrated in my locker and I grabbed it to read the message that had just come through.

HARPER

> Ava and I will be at The Lounge if you aren't doing anything.

A smile pulled on my lips and I sat back down on the bench as I typed out my response to her.

NICO

What time?

She must have been staring at her phone because she responded instantly.

HARPER

I have to go home first, so probably closer to 11.

It didn't give me much time to get ready, so I would just have to wear the suit I wore here to the bar. I would have exactly enough time to get a shower and head over there. The Lounge was only about ten minutes from the stadium, so half an hour was plenty of time.

NICO

I'll meet you there.

"The Lounge," Wes said from over my shoulder. I glanced back at him and found him standing there with a smirk on his face. "Who is Ava?"

I narrowed my eyes at him. "Do you understand privacy at all, bro? Who the fuck reads someone's messages over their shoulder?"

Lincoln laughed from where he was sitting as he overheard me scolding Wes. "You act like you don't know how he is."

Wes dropped down beside me. "Sorry, dude. You know I'm just nosy sometimes."

"Yeah, I know."

He was my best friend. I could never truly be mad at him or fault him for it. He didn't do anything with ill intent. Wes was just one of those goofy kind of people who was really his own person. He was nosy as hell, almost like he lived in a constant state of FOMO.

I stared at him for a moment. "You want to go along?"

Wes's face lit up and he tilted his head to the side. "Are you sure? I don't want to be, like, a third wheel or anything."

"It's not a date. Harper and I are just friends and she's going to be there with her friend, so it's not a date at all."

"Right, right," Wes said with a wink. "I need to get a shower and you know I'm down."

We split up, both of us focused on getting our gear put away so we could head into the showers. A part of me realized that maybe it wasn't a good idea inviting Wes along, but he could be trusted. If there was one person I trusted my life with other than G or my father, it was Wes.

He wouldn't tell anyone about Harper and I. Plus, we weren't going to be caught doing anything other than getting drinks tonight.

———

"Tell me about Ava," Wes said as we both walked from the parking lot toward the bar. "That's her name, right?"

"I'm pretty sure she has a boyfriend."

Wes chuckled. "Like that means anything."

I glanced at him from the corner of my eye. "Just don't."

He held his hands up in innocence. "Fine. I'll be on my best behavior and won't do anything with your girl's friend."

I glared at him. "She's not my girl."

"Right," he said with the sarcasm heavy in his tone as he rolled his eyes. "So, you wouldn't mind if she went home with someone else then tonight, right?"

My jaw clenched and ice slid through my gaze. Anger instantly sprung to life inside me and I swallowed it back. Wes was testing me and he knew exactly what he was doing. And goddamn him for being fucking right.

"Fucking liar," Wes mumbled as he held open the door for me to walk in ahead of him. The Lounge was busy when we got there and all of the tables were taken. As were the seats at the bar. There were people standing everywhere, practically crammed inside the building like a can of sardines.

It wasn't ideal but at the same time, it actually was. With this many people here, it wouldn't make it seem as obvious about being here with Harper. If anyone saw us here together, she would definitely be safe. After all, we didn't come here together. We were simply running into each other and having a drink.

As Wes and I pushed our way to the bar, I saw Harper sitting there with Ava. They were engaged in some kind of conversation and I didn't stop moving until I reached the back of her seat. My hands grazed the backs of her shoulders and she whipped her head in my direction.

I saw the wave of relief wash over her face as she saw that it was me. "Nico," she breathed, but it was hard to hear her over all the voices floating around the enclosed space. It was loud in the bar and I wanted to take her somewhere a little more private.

My eyes traveled over the top that she was wearing. It was a black, low-cut blouse that had two chain-like straps over her shoulders. Her blonde hair was pulled back in some kind of a twist, leaving her slender neck exposed. My dick was already hard just from looking at her.

"What do you guys want to drink?" Ava yelled over the noise to Wes and I. "I'm Ava," she introduced herself as she held out her hand.

I shook it gently. "Nico. I'll take a bourbon and ginger ale."

Wes did the same with a sly smirk pulling on his lips. "Wes. I'll take the same."

She narrowed her eyes at him. "I'll buy you a drink if you stop looking at me like you're going to take me home tonight. I'm already taken."

Harper laughed softly and I wanted to reach out and pluck it from the air and store it in my own personal collection of her sounds. Ava turned back around and waited for the bartender to order our drinks. Wes moved over to her and they struck up a conversation. He might have been known for being a playboy and talking a lot of shit, but that's exactly what it was. It was all talk.

"You played really well tonight," Harper told me as I hovered behind her.

I smiled as I dipped my mouth down to her ear. "It's because of you, love. Maybe we need to make a habit of seeing each other before games now too." I pulled back enough to see Harper's expression.

Her eyes were a bit hazy and she smiled back at me. "I think we could probably arrange that."

I raised an eyebrow after glancing at her drink that was half full. "How much have you had to drink? I don't think the Harper Jensen I know would willingly agree to something like that."

"Perhaps she had a change of heart," Harper said with a wink. "Maybe she realized that sometimes risks are worth taking."

My hand was still on the top of her back and I slowly moved it over her shoulder before dropping my mouth back to her ear. "I like the way that sounds."

Ava was suddenly leaning over toward the both of us with two shots. Wes was standing behind her with one in his hand. There was another guy with a shot too, who introduced himself as Ryan, Ava's boyfriend. Harper took one of the glasses and I followed suit, not quite sure what we were celebrating.

"To Harper!" Ava yelled out as she lifted her shot glass into the air. "I'm so proud of you and excited to see where your photography is taking you!"

We all tapped our shots together before swallowing back a mouthful of vodka. It burned my esophagus and I set my glass down as I looked at Ava. "What are we celebrating?"

Ava's eyes widened. "She didn't tell you? She has her first wedding shoot that she's going to be doing!"

My gaze dropped back to Harper's and she was avoiding looking at me as she drained the rest of her drink and slid the glass across the bar. Placing my hands on both of her shoulders, I leaned forward.

"Why didn't you tell me, love?" I probed, my attention solely on her. Thankfully the bar was still loud enough that no one could hear us. Ava was talking to her boyfriend and Wes disappeared to who the hell knew where.

Harper turned her head to face me until our cheeks were pressed against one another's. "I don't know. I didn't think it was something that was possible or would ever happen since most of my experience is in shooting sports."

"Don't you like sports photography?"

She shrugged. "I enjoy it, but I don't think it's where my heart is. I love love. I want to shoot engagements and weddings and babies. I don't want to spend my entire career shooting professional sports."

This was a complete game changer. I didn't want Harper to lose her job. Even though I could take care of her, she wanted to be independent. She made it clear that she couldn't afford to lose her job. But this really changed things. If she were to get established in doing what she truly loved, she could leave sports behind entirely. And then there would be nothing in the way of us.

"I love that for you," I told her as I pulled back and smiled down at the beautiful girl in front of me. "I know you will be amazing and it will all work out. If that is what you want to do, I know you will make it happen."

She stared at me for a moment, her eyes shining brightly at me. "How can you be so sure and so confident in me? It almost feels like it's a dream and it's literally only one shoot. It's not like I'm changing my career with this one job."

I drained the rest of my drink and set it down on the bar. "Because I believe in you, Harper. The sky is the fucking limit and there's nothing stopping you from achieving your dreams. I've seen how good your photography is. We just need to get it seen by the rest of the world."

"Who are you, Nico Cirone?" she breathed, her voice husky as she raked her teeth over her plump bottom lip.

I winked as I held my hand out to her. "Come with me and I'll show you."

"What about Ava?" she said as her eyes quickly searched mine with a touch of panic in them.

"Tell her whatever the fuck you need to, but you're leaving here with me." I paused as I pulled out my phone. "And we're leaving now."

She nodded and directed her attention to her friend as I sent Wes a text and told him that I was going to head out. He gave me a thumbs-up and nothing more, so I knew he was probably preoccupied or else he would have been digging for more details.

I took a few steps away, turning my back to the bar as I locked my screen and put my phone back into my pocket. As I pulled my keys from the same pocket, I felt a smaller hand slide into my other one. Turning my head, I glanced over and saw Harper standing beside me. Her chin was lifted as she looked up at me with a ghost of a smile playing on her lips.

"Are you ready to go?" I asked her over the crowd.

She nodded and smiled as she shifted her weight impatiently on her feet.

"My place or yours?"

"Mine is closer."

I smirked. She had the same thoughts as I did and I wasn't sure how much longer I'd be able to control myself around her.

"Your place it is."

Chapter Thirteen

Harper

I only had two drinks while I was at the bar and it felt like I was floating. It wasn't because of the alcohol. It was solely because of the man sitting in the driver's seat next to me with his hand wrapped around mine.

Nico Cirone was completely intoxicating. He was like a drug I couldn't get enough of. The more I was around him, the more I found myself missing him when I wasn't with him. He was like heroin in my veins. I wanted more of him, constantly chasing the high he gave me.

He muddled my thoughts and made my heart skip multiple beats. He probably wasn't good for my health and I had a feeling he definitely wasn't good for my heart. There was something different about him, yet I found myself questioning it all. When I first met him, he struck me as the playboy type with one thing on his mind.

The more time I spent with him, the more I realized that wasn't him at all.

There was so much more to Nico than he showed the world, and I wanted to peel back all of his layers. I wanted to know the real man behind the professional athlete persona. I wanted him to bury his secrets inside me.

His hand was warm against mine and he absent-mindedly stroked my skin with the pad of his thumb. When we got to his car, I gave him my address and he put it into his GPS so I didn't have to bother him with directions. It wasn't a far drive and it was literally only a few turns. The music was soft in the background, but all I could hear was the pounding of my heart.

As Nico pulled his car into the parking garage for my building, I couldn't help but feel a touch of anxiety. There was something about knowing that he was going to be in my space that had me feeling a little unpre-pared. It was one thing being at his place. If I went there or spent the night there, I was able to leave whenever I wanted to. Having him here was completely different. I couldn't run away from him and my feelings while he was in my own apartment.

He found an empty parking spot and parked his car in it before killing the engine. My hand was still in his and I fiddled with the strap of my purse on my lap.

"Harper." He spoke softly and his voice filled the empty space in the car. "Look at me."

I slowly turned my head to look at him. His eyes were filled with a touch of concern and he angled his head to the side.

"I don't have to come in if you don't want me to."

I stared back at him for a breath. "I want you to. It's just a little different for me, bringing someone back to my place instead of just going to yours."

Nico nodded in understanding, but he didn't let go of my hand. "We can sit out here for a little if you want."

"And do what?" I practically whispered the words as I turned in my seat to face him. It was dark in the car and the lights inside the garage seeped through the windows, making it just bright enough that I could make out his facial expression and features.

He shrugged. "Whatever you want."

I swallowed hard as the nervousness was mixing with the euphoric feeling he gave me. Something about the way he was looking at me had me feeling like the entire world was in my hands. Every choice was mine to make. I was the one who was controlling everything happening.

And I made my move. The one move I had never expected myself to actually have the guts to make.

Releasing his hand, I planted my own on his seat beside the headrest and I began to climb over the center console. Nico's seat was already slid back as far as it would go because of his long legs. He moved his arms out of the way and rested his hands on my hips as I straddled his lap.

He leaned his head back on the headrest and looked up at me with a look of curiosity mixing with the playful glimmer in his irises. "What are you up to, love?"

I placed both of my hands on his shoulders. "I want you, Nico. And I want you to fuck me in your car."

He raised an eyebrow at me. "Well, this is a different request. You'd rather I fuck you out here instead of in your apartment?"

I shook my head. "I want both." I paused for a moment, suddenly feeling a bit shy. "I've never had sex in a car before."

He studied me as a smile crept onto his lips. "Well, I would love to be your first."

Nico's hands were still around my waist and I stared down at him for a moment. There was something about being out here where anyone could walk out at any moment that had the adrenaline pumping through my veins. He slowly raised one hand to cup the back of my neck and pulled me down to him.

Our mouths collided and he stole the air from my lungs as his tongue slid against mine. He tasted like whiskey and he smelled like his soap. His hair was still damp from the shower he got before meeting us at the bar and I couldn't resist pushing my fingers through his tousled waves.

He started the kiss gentle, with his hands wandering beneath the bottom hem of my shirt. He pushed up the silk material and slid his hands beneath my bra as he rolled my nipples between his fingers. I couldn't stop myself as I moaned into his mouth and he swallowed the sound.

It only seemed to fuel him even more. The intensity of the need between us grew fiercely and it was suddenly a race to get undressed. I was lifting off his lap as he began to push his pants and underwear down. It was awkward as I dropped back into my own seat and kicked my shoes off.

Nico's eyes were dark with lust as his gaze collided with mine. He sat up and leaned over the center console as he pulled my pants and panties down, stripping me of the clothing that was covering up the bottom half of my body. There was nothing gentle about the way he gripped my hips and practically lifted me in the air before setting me back on his lap.

I lifted myself on my knees as he grabbed his cock and positioned it upright so the tip was pressed against me. As I lowered myself down on his length, he was stretching me to limits that felt almost impossible. I inhaled sharply, sucking in a breath as he filled me to the brim and I slid down until he was fully inside me.

Nico groaned, his fingertips were digging into my flesh as his eyes rolled back momentarily. "Jesus, fuck," he murmured as his hazy blues met mine. They were glazed over with need and his tongue darted out as he wet his lips. "You're so goddamn perfect, Harper."

Heat was building in the pit of my stomach as he stared up at me. I pressed my hands against his chest and he reached over to the side of the seat as he put the entire thing flat. I was hovering above him, completely in control now. I slowly began to move, working my hips as I lifted them off his lap before lowering myself back down.

"That's it, love," he growled, his eyes darkening as he helped move me. "Ride my cock like it's yours and no one else's."

We hadn't discussed whether or not we would be seeing or talking to other people. Hell, we didn't really have any conversations at all that had to do with what was going on between the two of us except the fact that no one could know. His words struck a chord of jealousy inside of me and it made me move my hips faster.

"There is no one else," I told him as I stared down at him. "No one rides this cock but me."

He nodded as mischief danced across his lips. "That's right, baby. No one but you. And fuck," he let out a low moan as I bounced on him faster, "you ride it so fucking well."

He abandoned one hip with his hand and slid it down between my legs. His fingers instantly found my clit and he began to work his thumb against my flesh. Nico was skilled with his hands, not only while holding a hockey stick, but also when they were between my thighs.

"Your pussy is clenched so tight around me right now," he groaned as he applied more pressure and worked his thumb faster. A sinister look danced in his irises as he abruptly slowed his movements. "You want to come, don't you? I can feel the way your body is beginning to tense and the way your breathing is quickening."

I nodded as I bit down on my bottom lip and continued to lift my hips as I slid up and down the length of his cock. "Yes, please," I moaned and practically pleaded. "Please let me come, Nico."

"You fuck my cock like you were made for it," he

said as he began to move his thumb again. "I want you to come for me, baby. Be a good girl and do it for me."

Between him deep inside me, the way that his thumb rolled around my clit, and his words, it didn't take long before I did exactly as he was asking of me. My orgasm tore through my body and I didn't stand a chance against the earthquake. My body felt like it was going to split in two and I would gladly fall apart for this man right now.

Nico's hands gripped my hips tightly and he took over as he fucked me from underneath. I was already riding a wave of ecstasy, practically paralyzed from the euphoric coma he had put me in. He pumped his hips a few more times before he was falling and crashing along with me.

He lost himself inside me and I collapsed against his chest as we were both riding out our highs. Nico released my hips and slid his arms up as he wrapped them around my body and held me close. We both still had our shirts on but I could feel his warmth radiating through our clothes. His touch was tender as he ran his palm across my shoulders.

I slowly pulled away and looked down at him. There was an indistinguishable look in his eyes but I couldn't seem to look away. It was as if he was staring directly into my soul, looking at nothing but my flesh and bones. Nico was slowly breaking down my walls and stripping away everything I had worked hard to build up to keep anyone out.

He was inside my veins.

And I was addicted.

Chapter Fourteen

Nico

Harper's apartment looked exactly like I thought it would. It was as if she plucked an entire board from Pinterest and brought it to life. It was very warm with neutral tones. There was no clutter and not a single item was out of place. She stepped inside her space and led me through the small area until we were walking into her bedroom.

Neither one of us had really said much since we exited my car. There was still a pink glow to Harper's cheeks and I couldn't help but smile to myself as I knew I was the reason behind the color on her face. It was an experience, having one of her firsts. But there was something more that happened in my car tonight.

There was a shift between us and we both felt it.

I tested her when I told her to ride my cock like it was hers and no one else's. I wanted to see how she reacted—and she took me by surprise. Part of me thought maybe she would stop and question me on it. Instead, it was like I lit a fire inside of her and she took exactly what she wanted. She made it clear that there was to be no one else.

Funny thing was, she didn't know that I only had eyes for her.

She was all I saw and no other women mattered except for her. There was no one who would ever compare to her and one day I would tell her how I truly felt. Until then, I needed to at least assure her that there was no one else. She would eventually realize that there would never be anyone but her.

She was it for me.

It shook me to my core, but I had never been this sure about anything else in my life before. It was like my soul just knew her. She fit into the missing pieces inside me. There was no other way I could explain it. It bordered on the line of obsession, but I knew in my heart it wasn't that. It was so much more—so much that I couldn't find an accurate word to fully describe it.

"I like your place," I told her as I lifted one arm and leaned against her doorway. Harper was already in her room, digging out a pair of sweatpants from her dresser.

She turned around to face me. "It isn't much, but it's enough for me."

"It is you," I smiled at her as I pushed off the doorway and stepped closer to her. "Warm and soft," I murmured as I brushed a piece of hair away from her face. "It just feels right. Like home."

Harper's lips parted and a soft breath escaped her as her eyes searched mine. We stood like that for a moment with my fingers lingering on the side of her face. She was the one who broke eye contact as she cleared her throat and took a step back, directing her gaze down to her feet.

"The remote is on the nightstand if you want to find something to watch," she told me as she grabbed the rest of her clothing to change into. "I'm just going to go into the bathroom and change into something a little more comfortable."

I moved my feet, stepping in front of her to block her way as I shook my head. "You don't need to hide from me, love."

"I'm not hiding from you," she lied through her teeth as she avoided my gaze and nervously shifted her weight.

"I was just inside you. I've seen you naked. I've tasted your pussy before." I paused for a moment as I slid my hand underneath her chin and lifted her chin to look up at me. "I don't want to leave, but if you don't want me to stay, I can go."

Her delicate throat bobbed as she swallowed and shook her head. "I don't want you to leave," she said softly, her voice half catching in her throat. "I want you to stay."

She took a step away from me and her eyes never left mine as she stripped down to nothing. I watched her as she slid on a new pair of underwear. Instead of putting on the other clothes she had in her hands, she dropped them to the floor and walked back to me.

Her gaze was still on mine as she slid the jacket away from my shoulders and it fell to the ground. She carefully slid each button through the hole it was in until she was pushing open my dress shirt. I cocked my head to the side as she pulled it away from my body.

"What are you doing, love?" I murmured as I trailed my fingertips along the side of her torso.

Harper smiled with a shy look dancing across her face as she took another step back and slid her own arms through the sleeves of my dress shirt. "I wanted your shirt instead of mine," she said with simplicity as she buttoned the shirt back up. "I hope that's okay."

I smiled back at her as I undid my pants and stepped out of them, leaving just my boxers on. "It looks better on you."

Harper climbed into her bed and I followed after her, sliding under the covers with her. She grabbed the remote and turned on the TV as she rolled onto her side. I moved behind her until my chest was pressed against her back and my arm was under her neck.

I nuzzled my face in the crook of her neck. "I can't get enough of you, Harper Jensen. I need you to know, there's no one but you."

She paused her search for a show and turned in my arms to face me. We were lying on the bed, face to face as she slid her leg over my own. "I know we haven't talked about it because I don't know what this even is between us. But I would like it if we didn't see other people while we're doing this."

A smirk played on my lips. "And what are we doing, exactly?"

She pulled her bottom lip between her teeth and I pulled it back out with my thumb. "I don't know," she whispered. "I can't put a label on it. I told you I wanted to take the risk, but it can't be anything official, you know? If we're ever questioned about it, I don't want to feel guilty denying it."

"So, you don't want a label, but you at least want it to be something exclusive?" I asked her as a spark of hope lit inside my heart. It was more than she had given me so far and I was willing to take whatever it was that Harper would give me.

She nodded. "I don't think I could handle it if I saw you with someone else."

I couldn't fight the smile that consumed me. "And why is that?"

"Because you're mine and no one else's."

My heart pounded erratically in my chest. "The same goes for you then, too. You're mine, Harper. I don't fucking share."

"You don't have to worry about that," she told me with a soft laugh. "You weren't even supposed to happen. I might have told you I wanted to forget about him, but you've done more than that already. You wiped him out of my memory completely."

"Sometimes life just has a way of inserting people into our lives without us asking for it." I rolled onto my back and pulled her close to me as we both looked at the TV. "I wasn't expecting you, Harper. You know the lifestyle that I live with my career. Yet, here you are, stuck in my fucking head. I've tried to get you out and I don't know how to."

"You're not the only one with that problem," she murmured, her lips brushing against my chest. "I think it's time we both stop trying to fight the inevitable."

I held her closer and traced invisible patterns on her back. "I promise I'll figure out a way so we can be together."

"Until then, no one can know but us."

"Well, I think Wes and Ava might have an idea if they don't already know," I reminded her as she slid her leg over my thighs.

"I forgot about them," she admitted quietly. "I know Ava won't say anything to anyone. Can Wes be trusted too?"

I nodded. "Absolutely. He's my best friend. I trust him completely." I paused for a moment. "You should know that I told my sister about you too, but she would never say anything to anyone."

Harper froze in my arms and she let out a breath before slowly pulling away from me. She sat up and turned to look at me with her eyes slightly wide. "Why did you do that?"

I didn't move from where I was laying in her bed. "Because my sister and I are close and I needed someone to talk to."

Harper's face softened and I watched the sympathy pass through her eyes. "I'm sorry. I just worry and if all these people know, it's only a matter of time before it gets out to more people. Stuff like this spreads like wildfire and then it's destroying an entire city."

I reached for her and wrapped my hands around her arms. She didn't fight me as I pulled her down on top of me and she propped her elbows on the bed as her chin hovered above my chest. Her eyes bounced back and forth between mine.

"What did your sister say?"

A soft chuckle rumbled in my chest. "That I better not fuck up your life and that you must be pretty special if I was talking to her about you."

A shy smile pulled on her lips and I grabbed the sides of her face as she tried to hide. She swallowed as she looked at me. A touch of seriousness shifted across her expression and I softly stroked her skin as I held her on top of me.

"It's true, Harper," I told her, my voice quiet. "I don't know what it is about you or what makes this different… but it is."

She folded her lips in between her teeth and slowly released them. "You know this is all going to blow up in our faces, right?" She let out a sigh and folded her hands on my chest before lowering her chin to rest on top of them. "Something like this is always too good to be true. We talk about how no one will find out, but there's a part of me that just refuses to believe that. The truth always comes out."

"It will all be okay. I will do everything to protect you. I will lie to whoever I need to, to make sure no one finds out." I stared directly at her crystal blue eyes. "You know that, right? I would never let anything happen to you or your job. I might not be able to stay away from you, but I can keep this a secret. I can make sure no one else will ever find out."

"But the people who already know… how can we be so sure they won't say anything?"

A smile pulled on my lips. "Because they value their lives."

Harper's eyes widened slightly. "You wouldn't do that."

"I would consider it," I told her with a shrug. "They would never do something like that."

"If you believe it, then I have no reason not to believe it too."

She stared back at me with nothing but trust in her eyes, and I knew in that moment that whatever this was between us was something fucking sacred. It was something I would protect at all costs, just like I would protect her.

Harper Jensen scared the living shit out of me... because I was fairly certain I was falling in love with her.

Chapter Fifteen

Harper

As I stood inside the bridal suite, I took pictures of the bride and all of her bridesmaids while they were getting their hair and makeup done. Leila, the bride, looked absolutely stunning in her white lace dress and her mother stood behind her as they stared into the mirror. I snapped a few shots of them as they had a private conversation between one another.

It was such a sweet moment, watching the tender moments between a daughter and her mother as she got ready to walk down the aisle to marry the man she chose to spend the rest of her life with. Standing in the background as I observed and took candid photos, I realized I would never have these moments in sports photography.

There was a part of me that loved the action and the excitement. Every game was adrenaline-fueled and it was impossible to not feel the energy. It was high stress and much more demanding than something like this.

You got to witness amazing moments while photographing a game, but nothing compared to something like this.

There just weren't words that quite described it in a way that would do it justice.

Watching Leila and her mother made me realize that this was the career move I needed to make. It was my first official shoot like this, but if I were able to impress them, then it would only help to build my portfolio and résumé.

When I first got into photography, it was always my goal to have my own business. I wanted to be the one in control and capture moments in time like a wedding or a birth. Different lifelong milestones that people would look at the pictures for years to come. Sports photography was just something I got into almost by accident.

It started when I was in college and I needed something to get started with. That's how I ended up shooting sports and primarily hockey. It just built from there and I was riding the path, even though it wasn't the one I was destined to be on.

"Harper, would we be able to get some shots of Evan when Leila comes walking down the aisle?" Leila's mother asked me as she walked over in her soft coral dress.

They had hired me but asked that I bring someone else along with me because they wanted to have images from every possible angle. There was no way I would have been able to capture everything they wanted just by myself, so I asked Ava if she would come with me. I didn't have a team; I didn't have an established business.

Ava was more than happy to come along. She knew this was my dream and she only wanted the best for me. This was all such a great learning experience, but I now knew that if I were going to start my own business, I would need to have someone for situations like this.

"Absolutely. I will make sure to get some of him and Leila walking down the aisle to him," I assured her with a smile. "I'll also make sure to take some of the ceremony from that angle and side as well."

"That sounds perfect." She smiled back at me and nodded. The bridal party gathered around the bride and I took one last picture of them before heading out to where the ceremony would be.

They were having it at an upscale hotel that had a room they were able to transform into one they could hold a ceremony in. It was amazing the way they had everything set up. It didn't even feel like you were in a hotel, but almost as if it were somewhere ethereal with the flowers and glowing lights around.

Everyone was already in their seats waiting and I found a spot I had chosen earlier in the day that I felt would give me a good angle for these shots. Evan was standing at the front of the room with his groomsmen lined up alongside of him. I spotted Ava and waved to her. She was set up in a position where she would get Leila as she walked down the aisle, along with the ceremony from her side of the room.

A few minutes had passed and we were waiting for everyone to be in place and the music to shift. My phone vibrated in my pocket and I knew I had a moment to spare, so I pulled it out and checked my messages.

NICO

I know I told you good luck earlier, but I realized that wasn't appropriate. You don't need luck. You're amazing and you are going to nail this job.

His message warmed my soul and I reread it three times while trying to calm my heart in my chest. Nico Cirone seemed like a smooth talker, but he actually meant the words he spoke. I hadn't seen him in a few days, but he was the first text I woke up to and the last I went to sleep to every night. He was the best part of my day and I found myself missing him when I didn't get to see him.

HARPER

Thank you. I will let you know how it goes afterward. The ceremony is about to start now.

He responded immediately.

NICO

I can't wait to hear about it :)

I smiled down at my phone in my hand just as the music shifted into the song that Leila picked to walk down the aisle to. I quickly got my camera into position and zoomed in to focus on Evan and no one but him.

His face cracked as his bride stepped into the aisle.

My shutter flickered as I pressed down on the button in rapid succession. I couldn't stop the smile from pulling my lips upward as I watched Evan fight his emotions until the tears were springing from his eyes.

Leila joined him at the front of the room and the ceremony commenced. I moved around, taking pictures of their special day from various angles. I was pretty sure everyone was crying by the time the ceremony was over. They wrote their own vows and the love between them was something to be envious of. It was what everyone was looking for and it was radiating from them, drifting across the room in waves.

After the ceremony, I went to take pictures of the bridal party while Ava got set up in the reception room. The positive energy was contagious and I felt myself moving along to the music as we took pictures of everyone dancing during the reception. Leila's mother found Ava and I and told the two of us that there were plates of food for us at one of the tables and that we needed to take a break.

Ava and I got ourselves drinks from the bar and found our spots at the table Leila's mother directed us to. I looked over at my friend who was wearing the biggest smile as she watched everyone out on the dance floor.

"I think Ryan is going to propose," she mused out loud as she looked over at me. "He's been acting really strange and nervous around me lately. My sister said he stopped by to talk to our parents, which I found strange. There's no reason why he would be there without me unless it was something he didn't want me to know about."

I stared at her for a moment as I smiled. "This is amazing, Ava. Have you guys talked about it at all?"

She shrugged. "I mean, yeah, but nothing in depth. I don't know. He weirdly asked me to go to dinner with him next Friday night, which seems weird too. Like, since when do we need to plan ahead for a date?"

"Oh my god." My eyes widened as everything she was saying was pointing in the direction she was thinking. "He's definitely going to ask you. This feels like something straight out of a movie."

"I feel like I could vomit," she said with a laugh as she shook her head. "I mean, not about saying yes or anything, but like the anticipation. He's either going to propose or break up with me."

"He's definitely going to propose," I assured her. "Everyone sees the way he looks at you. He's obsessed. He's not breaking up with you."

Ava turned to face me and raised an eyebrow. "Speaking of obsessed… Nico Cirone?!"

I grimaced in an attempt to hide the way my lips were curling upward and I ducked my head. "I know, I know. You can't say anything to anyone, though."

"He's the guy from the club that night too, isn't he?"

I looked back up at her and nodded. "I didn't want to say anything because that was obviously just something random. But yeah… we've been hanging out and talking since then."

"I can't believe you didn't tell me!" she said loudly before taking a sip of her drink. "I mean, I can understand why you wouldn't want anyone to know, but shit. He's fucking hot as hell and I'm your best friend."

"I'll lose my job if anyone finds out about it and I can't afford to lose it right now."

Ava nodded and fell silent as she looked around the room. "What if you didn't have to work for the Vipers anymore? What if you could make your dreams come true and do this full-time instead?"

I looked at her as I chewed on the inside of my cheek. "I mean, that's what my goal is. There's no guarantee that it will happen or work out. Working for the Vipers right now is a sure thing. That's what pays my bills, and I can't jeopardize that."

"Tonight is obviously going so well. If we can use this to get the ball rolling, you're going to have people calling you all the time." Ava pulled out her phone. "My cousin is due in, like, two weeks to have a baby. I'm forcing her to book a newborn shoot with you." She looked up at me and her eyes were wide. "And my one friend who is getting married. The photographer she originally hired recently backed out, so she's going to need you too."

"Ava," I started as I shook my head at her. "You can't just force all of these people to hire me."

She waved her hand dismissively. "Nonsense. I'm not forcing them. It's all word of mouth. You're a talented photographer and we're going to make this happen for you." She smirked and winked. "That way you don't have to be Nico Cirone's dirty little secret."

"I'm not his dirty little secret," I argued as I lifted my glass to my mouth.

Ava nodded. "You're right. He's *your* little secret."

I almost spat my drink out and half choked on it as I swallowed down the liquid and laughed. "Oh my gosh, Ava," I laughed as I shook my head at her. "That sounds so bad."

"Tell me I'm wrong."

"You're not," I said as we both giggled. We quickly finished eating as the wedding began to shift again and it was time for the two of us to get back to work.

As much as I didn't want her pushing my work on other people, I was excited for the possibilities. For the different jobs and making my dreams come true.

But more importantly, I was excited for what this could do for Nico and I.

He wouldn't have to be my secret anymore…

Chapter Sixteen

Nico

Shifting my weight on my feet, I checked the time on my phone again. Harper told me about twenty minutes ago that she was leaving the venue. She should be here any minute. I couldn't help but feel a little awkward standing outside of her door with a bouquet of flowers. I didn't tell her I was going to be coming by and I suddenly felt nervous about being here.

What if she didn't want to see me? Was it weird that I came here with flowers like she just won an award? I was insanely proud of her for chasing after her dreams and making a name for herself. I just wanted to show my support and this was the first thing that came to my mind.

Movement from down the hall caught my attention and I looked down to see Harper walking toward me with her bags of equipment. She was wearing a light gray dress that hugged her curves in all the right places. Her black heels clicked against the floor beneath her feet and I couldn't stop my eyes from trailing along her bare legs.

Fuck. She was breathtaking.

Harper fumbled with the keys in her hands and her eyes bounced to mine as she let out a gasp. "Nico," she said breathlessly as a wave of confusion passed through her irises. "You scared me. What are you doing here?"

Her eyes dropped down to the flowers and then back up to meet my gaze. A pink tint spread across her cheeks and she instinctively batted her eyelashes at me.

"Here," I said to her as I reached for her bags while handing her the flowers. "Let me carry those and you take these."

She didn't argue as she slid the straps from her shoulders and I took them from her. She looked down at the flowers in her hands and back up to me. "What are these for?"

"Just because," I told her with a shrug as she unlocked her apartment door and let me in with her. "I wanted to surprise you and let you know how proud I am of you."

Harper paused just inside her apartment as she turned to look at me. "You got me 'just because' flowers? And showed up at my place to surprise me?"

I swallowed roughly over the walnut-sized lump that formed in my throat and nodded. "I did," I said quietly, not fully trusting my voice.

The look in her eyes was a mixture of surprise and contentment. No words needed to be spoken between us in that moment. The meaning behind the flowers shook me to the core and it wasn't until she questioned me on it that the reality of the situation hit me in my fucking soul. I didn't just go out and buy people flowers.

"The only person I've ever bought flowers for before was my mother," I told her with nothing but pure honesty. My voice was barely audible and Harper's eyes searched mine. "The last ones I bought were a week before she passed away."

Harper's eyes were soft and I watched the moisture collect on her lashes. She took the bags from me and set them on a bench that she had by the entrance. She stepped closer to me, wrapping her arms around my torso as she pressed herself flush against my body.

Instinctively, I wrapped my arms around the tops of her shoulders and held her close as I buried my face in her hair. It wasn't often that I allowed the grief to settle in, but I couldn't help myself right now. There was something about the moment that had a rush of feelings slamming into my chest. My heart constricted and I blinked back the tears.

I had already grieved the loss of my mother, but those damn flowers. They had emotions rushing back to me in a moment and I needed to focus on Harper. She was the one who could ground me in this moment.

"Thank you for the flowers," she murmured against my shirt as she held me tightly. "They're beautiful."

I slowly pulled back from her and she leaned her head back to look up at me. "Then they're perfect for you. You deserve everything in the fucking world and I want to be the one who gives it to you."

She stared back at me. "Nico…"

"Shh," I shushed her as I lifted a finger to press to her lips. "You don't need to argue with me. I won't say anything more. I just want you to know that you're important to me, okay? And I'm so goddamn proud of you. You had the opportunity to explore another avenue in your career and you killed it."

She laughed quietly and shook her head in disbelief. "You haven't even seen any of the images, so how could you possibly say that?"

"Because I know you," I smiled down at her, "and you are nothing short of amazing."

Her eyes were bright as she stared into my soul. Harper Jensen had crawled her way through my veins and into my heart. She nestled herself deep inside and made it her home. Harper was my home and I never wanted to be without her.

"Let me take you out. We need to go celebrate this tonight."

"Tonight?" She glanced at the clock on the wall. "Isn't it getting kind of late?"

I shrugged. "I guess it depends on where you want to go."

"What did you have in mind?"

I held up the bottle of champagne I brought over for her. "Grab two glasses and I know of somewhere we can go where we don't have to worry about them closing."

Harper eyed me skeptically, but I didn't miss the excitement in her eyes. She pushed away from me and went into her kitchen before coming back with two glasses. I slid my hand into hers and laced our fingers together before I pulled her back out of her apartment.

She didn't question me as I led her to my car. She held on to my hand as we headed through the city until we were leaving the city limits. It wasn't a far drive to the lake and I parked my car under a canopy of trees by the one dock. Harper looked over at me with a tender smile as I got out of my car.

She followed suit and met me around the front of the vehicle. She was still wearing the dress from earlier and the night air was cold. I watched her for a moment as she wrapped her arms around herself and rubbed her arms. Grabbing the back of my hoodie, I pulled it over my head and handed it to her.

Harper looked up at me. "You're going to be cold."

A chuckle rumbled in my chest and I shook my head at her. "Don't worry about me, love. Put it on. We won't be out here long. I don't want to risk you freezing."

Harper's hand was back in mine and I led her to the bench by the dock. Out here, there weren't many lights and we had a perfect view of the stars scattered in the sky above us. Had I thought about this more in depth, I would have brought a blanket or something to make us more comfortable. Instead, this was all on the fly.

Harper held both of the glass flutes in her hands and I popped open the champagne. The sound of her laughter slid across my eardrums like silk as I poured some of the bubbly liquid into each glass. I set the bottle down onto the ground and held my drink into the air.

"To you, my love," I said with a smile as I stared into her bright blue eyes. "The sky is the limit for you and your dreams. I can't wait to see where this will take you and I'm so proud of you for trying something you've always wanted to do."

She stared at me for a moment as emotion welled in her eyes. Her tongue darted out to wet her lips and she tapped her glass to mine. We both took a sip and I slid my arm around the tops of her shoulders, pulling her flush against my side. Harper leaned her head back and rested it on my bicep as she looked up at the night sky.

"How do you always know the right things to do and say?"

My eyes trailed over the side of her face, memorizing her facial features. She looked angelic with the way the moon cast its light across her cheek. Everything about her was perfect and no one could ever tell me otherwise. It was like an angel had reached down from the heavens and handcrafted her.

"I don't," I told her quietly. "I just say whatever I'm feeling when it comes to you. The things that I say to you—they're words that were made just for you and no one else."

She slowly sat up and turned to look at me. "Why me, though? You could literally have anyone else on this stupid planet, yet you chose me."

"And I'll always choose you," I told her as I slid my hand to the base of her neck. "I don't want anyone else, Harper. I know things are complicated but I don't give a shit."

Harper's eyes shimmered under the light of the moon. She fell silent and I pulled her back against my side. She shifted her body and tucked her legs up on the bench underneath her. Her arm snaked its away around my torso and she rested her head on my chest.

"My mom would have loved you," I said as I gently stroked her long silky hair. "I wish she could have been around to meet you."

"Tell me about her."

A smile began to bloom as I allowed my mind to drift into those happier thoughts. Not the ones about her being gone, but the memories of when she was here. When things were simpler in life. When she was still around, acting as the glue that held our family together. Before our father became a shell of a person and Giana and I were the only ones who really had each other anymore.

"She was so caring and loving. She was always cracking jokes and thought that she was the funniest. There wasn't a single thing she missed. Between my sister and I, she had spread herself so thin, but you could never tell. She was always on the sidelines cheering both of us on in life." I paused for a moment as my heart ached. "She never had a mean thing to say about anyone, but if someone said anything about either of us, she went into momma bear mode."

"She would be really proud of you, Nico."

My smile fell a bit. "I would like to think she would. She was around to see me get drafted, but she never got to see me play professionally. She was the one who was waking up before the sun when I was a kid, making sure I was getting to practice and tournaments on time. She was the definition of a hockey mom and she never complained about it—well, not to me at least."

"I'm sorry she didn't get to see you play. I'm sure her getting to see you get drafted was an amazing experience for her," Harper offered, her voice soft and gentle as she held me a little tighter. "She's always with you, Nico."

I swallowed back the emotion that built in my throat and nodded. "I know she is. I just wish she were physically here too, you know? I wish she could have met you," I repeated my earlier sentiment.

"I wish I could have had the chance to meet her."

I held Harper for a little longer as we watched the stars shine above us. She shivered in my arms and I knew it was time for us to get out of here. "Let's get you somewhere warm, love."

Harper rose from the bench and I followed along with her after grabbing the empty glasses and the half-empty bottle of champagne. She smiled at me as she slid her hand into mine and I led her back to my car. She fell asleep as I drove back to her place and when I parked in front of her building, I couldn't tear my eyes away from her.

She was exactly where she belonged—right beside me with her hand in mine.

And I was going to do whatever I had to, to make sure that was exactly where she stayed.

Chapter Seventeen

Harper

"Thank you so much, Phillip!" I said into the speaker of the phone as I paced up and down the hallway in Nico's apartment. He had jumped into the shower when my phone rang and when I saw who was calling, I knew I had to pick it up.

"I will have everything arranged and you'll fly out with the team on Friday morning," Phillip told me.

I smiled, feeling the excitement building within me. I was so thrilled to get invited to go along and shoot their away game. It wasn't an opportunity that everyone was given and here I was, getting the invitation from my boss. "What city are they playing in?"

"Vegas," Phillip answered and my stomach instantly sank. "I gotta go, Harper. But I will see you at the game."

He abruptly ended the call and I slowly lowered my phone away from my face. I didn't want to go to Vegas. The last time I was there was when Connor broke up with me. Being in the city wasn't what actually bothered me, though. What bothered me was going to the same arena he played in. Nico's team was going to be playing his and we were going to be in their territory.

The bathroom door opened and steam billowed out as I lifted my head to look up at Nico. He stood there, his body still damp with a towel wrapped around his waist. I watched him, my mouth dry as he crossed his arms and leaned against the doorway.

"What's wrong?"

I swallowed hard and shook my head. "Phillip wants me to go on the road with you guys and shoot your next away game."

Nico's face lit up. "That's fucking awesome, Harper! You can come travel with me, we can check out the city. It will be like a little getaway, kind of."

I tried to match his enthusiasm, but I couldn't. My smile didn't quite reach for the sky like his did. I watched as his fell and his eyebrows pulled together.

"You don't seem excited."

I ran my hand over my forehead and looked back at him. "My ex plays for the Bruisers."

Nico's face transformed between a mixture of rage and relaxation. "Wait... you didn't tell me your ex played in the NHL too. Who is it?"

I let out a sigh and muttered his name, "Connor Davenport." My heart pounded in my chest. "I'm over him, he doesn't matter to me, but he's a fucking asshole and I don't want to have to see him again. At least not there."

"So, it would be different for you if he was playing here?"

I nodded. "This is my home. My territory."

The corners of Nico's lips twitched. "I like that." He pushed away from the doorway and closed the distance between us until he was caging me in with his hands on the wall on either side of my head. "Fuck him. Come with me anyways."

I tilted my head to the side. "You know I'm not actually coming with you, though, right? I have to stay in my own room away from you."

Nico laughed softly. "That's just a formality, love. You know I'll come find you when it's safe."

Ecstasy surged through my system as he dropped his hand to cup the side of my face. Like a hit to my veins, he was racing through my body and I couldn't get enough of him. There was no rehab to help get over my addiction to Nico Cirone. I was completely fucked and there was no way I would ever recover from him.

"I don't want to see him."

Nico stared down at me as a shadow passed through his expression. "You let me worry about him."

My lips pursed and I gave him a knowing look. "Promise me you won't start anything with him. Just let it go. If he were to find out about the two of us, I wouldn't put it past him to try and effectively ruin my life."

He raised an eyebrow at me. "Why are you afraid of him, love? What did he really do to you?"

I swallowed hard over the emotion that welled in my throat. "He was just really controlling. He wasn't happy when I refused to move cities with him and he made it known. He tracked my every movement and didn't say the nicest things to me about it. When he finally gave me an ultimatum and I declined, it was like watching a volcano erupt. He was usually kind, although I had seen his ugly side a time or two before. When things got bad, they got really bad."

Nico's eyes grew dark. "Did he hurt you?"

I shook my head. "Not really."

"What did he do to you, Harper?"

I closed my eyes as the memories flooded my mind. "He never laid a finger on me. He was unkind with his words and our fights were never pretty. It was a messy relationship and a messy breakup. He threw a glass at me one night." I sucked in a deep breath as I lifted the hair away from my forehead to show him the small scar. "That was the last fight we ever had."

Nico fell silent and he moved my hand out of the way as he replaced it with his own. I opened my eyes to look at him, but he wasn't looking at me. His attention was solely focused on the scar on my forehead. He gently rubbed his thumb across it as his eyes found mine. A storm was brewing in his eyes, yet there was a tenderness reserved just for me.

He cupped both sides of my face and pressed his lips against my scar. "I want to snap his fucking neck," he growled against my skin. "He's going to pay for hurting you."

"Nico, please," I pleaded with him as my voice caught in my throat. "I've already closed that chapter of my life. Just let it go."

Nico pulled away and looked down at me. His stormy eyes pierced mine. "I can't let it go, Harper. He hurt you. You, of all fucking people." He took a breath, his chest rising as his nostrils flared.

I shook my head at him. "It's in the past. Please, just leave it there." My eyes searched his with desperation. "He's insignificant in my life, Nico. I'd like to leave things like that."

His jaw clenched and his eyes fell shut. I watched him carefully as he sucked in a deep breath, his chest puffing out as his lungs expanded. He held it in for a beat before slowly exhaling and opening his eyes back up to look at me. "I will let it go, but only because you asked me to."

Nico's words were convincing, but there was something in his eyes that had me questioning the sincerity of it.

"I need you to promise me you won't say anything to him."

"I promise, love," he said with a nod. He raised an eyebrow. "I won't say anything, but I can't promise he won't get slammed into the boards."

I pursed my lips. Hockey was already an aggressive sport. I knew how it worked when someone had an issue with another player. Asking Nico to not check him or anything was like asking a fish to not swim in water. "Please don't make it anything too obvious."

Nico smirked. "Never."

His hands slowly traveled down my body as he slid them under the bottom hem of my shirt. I raised my arms up as he lifted the piece of clothing up and over my head before tossing it onto the floor. "So, does that mean you'll come along with me?"

"I'll go along with the team," I told him with a playful tone. "I'm not coming with you."

A chuckle vibrated in his chest as he buried his face in my neck. "You will be soon enough."

I didn't have a bra on and his hand instantly cupped my breast. My hands were trailing down his torso, pushing his towel away and it pooled around his feet on the floor. His lips found mine in a rush and he swiftly stole the air from my lungs as he breathed me in.

Nico surrounded me and consumed me with his touch and his mouth. He stripped me down to my bones and buried himself deep within my marrow. He was in my soul and there was no way to eradicate him.

His fingers hooked under the waistband of my panties and he pushed them down my legs as his mouth traveled across the planes of my body. As he stood back up in front of me, he hooked his arms under the backs of my legs and lifted me into the air. Nico pushed deep inside me with one thrust.

My back was against the wall, my nails were gripping at his shoulders, and he gripped my hips as he thrust into me. He slid in and out of me, pounding into me harder each time. My body felt like it was going to split in half, like we were going to break through the wall behind me.

A fire started in the pit of my stomach and was quickly spreading through my body like wildfire. Nico was in my veins and I was chasing the high. *He was my high.* His mouth was on mine, swallowing my moans while our ragged breaths mixed together. We were climbing and climbing with each thrust.

"Come with me, love," Nico whispered against my lips as he thrust harder into me.

It didn't take long before we were both falling off the edge of the cliff together, falling into an abyss of ecstasy. He didn't stop moving inside me until we were both riding the waves of our orgasms. He pulled his face away from mine, his bright blue eyes piercing my own.

"I'm so fucking lost in you, Harper," he breathed with something heavy lingering in his irises. "You have no idea what you do to me."

I stared back at him with the words stuck in my throat like peanut butter. He slowly pulled out of me, but instead of setting me down on the ground, he carried me back to his bedroom and laid me on the sheets. He paused at the edge of the bed, his gaze trained on my eyes as he watched me for a moment.

He was wrong. I knew exactly what I was doing to him, because he was doing the same exact thing to me.

I was just as lost in him.

Chapter Eighteen

Nico

As I stepped onto the ice for warm-ups, I circled around half of the rink we were at. I followed behind Wes, my legs powering as I pushed off with my opposite leg with each stride. The muscles in my thighs contracted, but I didn't feel the burn I would feel later on during the game. Skating around the right side of the net, I spotted Harper where she was setting up.

She was testing out her camera with the lens just barely through the small cutout in the glass. She lifted her head and a soft smile touched her lips as she noticed me. I smiled back at her and winked as I skated past. I watched pink hues touch her cheeks as she ducked her head back to her equipment.

I snuck into her hotel room in the middle of the night. We didn't get in until late last night and I couldn't get away from Wes until he passed out. We had to be up early for workouts so I just woke up an

173

hour earlier than everyone else so I could stop in and see her.

When I left her room in the morning to get ready to meet the rest of the guys, she slipped me the extra key to her room with the same pink hues on her cheeks. I smiled to myself as I skated around and slid a puck along the ice with the blade of my stick.

Wes came up to me, bumping his shoulder into mine. "You're awfully smiley today," he said in a thoughtful tone. "I wonder why that is."

I gave him a sideways glance. "No idea what you're talking about," I mumbled."

"Mhm," Wes mused as a smirk pulled on his lips. He quickly stole the puck from me. "I'm sure it doesn't have anything to do with a certain someone who came along for the trip."

I stole the puck back and skated away from him without another word. As I sent the puck toward Wolfe, he blocked my shot with his blocker and I circled around. My eyes traveled across the ice and as soon as I saw him, I saw fucking red.

Number 14. Davenport.

I wanted to fucking kill him. Call me irrational or whatever the hell you wanted to. He hurt someone who I cared about. That was grounds for making him pay for it. Harper begged me not to say anything and I never would; I'd never do something that would draw any attention to what was going on between us.

She asked me not to do anything too obvious, and I wouldn't. The last thing I wanted to be was a threat to her. But Davenport... he was a fucking threat. He had already proved himself to be a piece of shit and I couldn't shake the feeling that was crawling underneath my skin. I narrowed my eyes as I assessed him from the blue line.

One way or another, he was going to pay for what he did to her.

The ten-minute warm-up flew past and before I knew it, we were back in the locker room while the Zamboni cut the ice. Everyone was double-checking their gear, making sure everything was in place and ready to go. My mind was in a daze, but not the good kind. It was actually a conflicting feeling.

I was thrilled that Harper was on the road with us. I loved her being along for the trip and the experience. That, and it was another great thing to add to her résumé. But then there was the part of me that couldn't stop thinking about Davenport and how badly I wanted to end his career tonight.

"Cirone, let's go!" Mac yelled at me from where he was standing in line. I was supposed to be in front of him, yet I was still lingering by my locker, trying to get my shit together.

I walked over to where he was and we all got our gloves on. Everyone began to file out and I grabbed my stick from Miles and headed out onto the ice. Coach moved me to the first line, so I took off my helmet and stood where I was supposed to while the national anthem was sung.

Shifting my weight back and forth on my skates, I kept my head down until it was time for us to get into position for the start of the game. As I skated to the center of the rink and placed my stick against the ice, I saw Harper's ex. He was on the same line as me. We didn't play the same position but he was right fucking there.

My jaw clenched and I fought the urge to charge at him at that moment. As the puck dropped, I shifted my focus away from him and played my ass off instead. I channeled all of my aggression into playing the best game of hockey I could play.

As we got into the third period, tensions were high between everyone. We were tied 2-2 and it was a pretty even matchup between our team and theirs. Everyone was dead-ass tired, but we still had to keep pushing on. It wasn't a loss that we were going to hand over to them, and it wasn't one they were willing to give up either.

There were only three minutes left in the last period of the game. We were quickly approaching overtime territory, but in such a fast game like hockey, things could easily change within a matter of seconds. And that was exactly what happened.

Their center had a breakaway. He managed to get the puck away from our team and he turned and started power skating toward our net. I was tangled up with their left winger and it took me a fraction of a second to get away from him. By the time I did and skated after the rest of the guys moving down the ice, I was too fucking late.

He managed to snipe a shot right past Wolfe. The buzzer sounded loudly through the entire arena and the defeat hung heavily through the air. Slowing down on my skates, I watched as he celebrated, but he wasn't the only one. Davenport skated directly over to the boards, right where Harper was positioned with her camera.

It was as if time slowed down as he jumped into the air, his hip slamming against the glass in celebration for a goal he didn't even score. It was completely out of pocket and my breath caught in my throat as I watched Harper stumble backward. Instantly, I skated as hard and as fast as I could in their direction. As I approached them, I noticed Harper's camera wasn't in her hands and as Davenport moved out of the way, I saw the blood dripping from her nose as she covered her face with her palms.

Davenport looked over at her with a look of satisfaction on his face. My blood fucking boiled and I couldn't stop the rage as it began to race through my veins. All I wanted to see was his blood on the ice and my hands and nothing was going to stop me now. The promise I made Harper was out the window. This wasn't the first time he hurt her and it may have looked like an accident to everyone else, but I fucking knew.

He did that on purpose and the look on his face only solidified that. And that was all I needed to charge straight in his direction. My feet didn't stop moving until I was coming up on him. Just as he turned around to face me, I lifted my stick with both hands and cross-checked him in the chest, sending him back into the boards.

"What the fuck was that for, bro?" he shouted at me as he threw his stick and gloves onto the ice. "You've been running at me all fucking night."

I followed his lead, throwing my own gloves and stick onto the ice, but I was already one step ahead of him. He didn't even have a chance to come at me as I grabbed a fistful of the collar of his jersey and the top of his chest protector. I yanked him toward me and drove my fist directly into the side of his face. The rage behind the blow had enough force to instantly knock him out.

His entire body went limp and I let go of him as his body crumpled onto the ice. My eyes were no longer on him. I didn't give two shits about him and if we weren't in a professional setting right now, I would have followed him down onto the ice with my fists meeting his face until he was unidentifiable. I skated over to the glass where Harper was.

She was sitting on the concrete steps and there were a few people around checking on her. I watched as she held a bloodied napkin under her nose. She lifted her eyes, looking up at me with tears in them. I wanted to break through the glass to get to her, but I couldn't. It was fucking killing me not being able to be with her and I couldn't stand here any longer or I'd be drawing attention to the two of us.

Spinning around on my skates, I saw Connor Davenport shakily rising to his feet and a few of his guys were helping to steady him as they skated him over to their bench. We had both gotten penalties and there was no sense in staying out for the remainder of the game since we'd be in the box anyway.

I headed back to the locker room with only one thing on my mind: I needed to get the fuck out of here and get to her. I quickly undressed, showered, and put my dress clothes back on before the guys came back in from the game.

Disappointment hung heavily in the air as they all filed in and I couldn't stop my foot from bouncing off the floor as I impatiently waited. Looking down at my phone, I found Harper's name and opened up our message thread.

NICO

Tell me you're okay, love.

My jaw clenched and I stared at my screen. I waited for her response, but nothing came through. It was quite literally killing me. I hung my head as I locked my screen and picked at the scab that was forming on my knuckles from where I had cut them on Connor's helmet.

"I saw what happened," Wes said quietly as he sat down next to me, smelling like sweat and hockey gear. "He's lucky you knocked him out with one hit."

I looked over at my best friend. "He's her ex."

Wes's eyes widened. "Oh, fuck. So, what he did wasn't an accident."

I shook my head in confirmation. "I need to see her."

"I know, man," he said with a frown. "We'll be out of here soon enough. No one said anything about going out, so I'll cover for you when we get back to the hotel if needed."

"Thanks, bro. I appreciate you."

Wes shrugged. "It's what I'm here for."

My phone vibrated in my hand and I quickly turned

my attention away from Wes as I unlocked the screen. Harper responded and my heart skipped a beat in my chest.

HARPER

I'm okay.

I sighed a breath of relief, yet I wasn't fully convinced. I needed to see for myself that she was actually okay. It wasn't that I didn't believe her, the whole situation was jarring and I had a feeling Harper was going to be shook-up from it. Anyone in their right mind would have been, especially with getting a camera slammed into their face.

There was only one thing that mattered to me at that moment.

I needed to see her.

Chapter Nineteen

Harper

Sitting with my legs crisscrossed on the bed, I slowly removed the bag of ice away from my face. I could see my reflection in the mirror across from me and I winced at the bruises that were beginning to develop underneath my eyes. The bleeding thankfully stopped by the time I got to the team's medical staff.

After the doctor assessed my nose, he determined that it wasn't broken, just that there was a decent amount of inflammation from the trauma. He could almost guarantee there would be significant bruising and swelling that could last a week or more. My nose took the brunt of the blow, but because of the way it hit my nose, I was going to end up sporting two black eyes.

I wasn't expecting Connor to do something like that. It was clearly intentional, considering the fact that he had been subtly fucking with me during the game. I didn't miss the way Nico kept targeting him, but

Connor either blocked my opportunities for shots or even went as far as sending a puck in my direction.

It was hard to tell for sure if it was accidental or not but I saw the way he looked at me each time he did something. Or he skated away with a smirk. When he jumped against the glass, his hip slammed into my camera that was still positioned through the small cutout.

I didn't have time to move away, as my face was still against the camera. The force slammed it directly into my face, knocking me backward. I fumbled my camera and wasn't able to catch it before it fell to the ground. The concrete was no match for the lens and it was now cracked.

The initial blow to my nose had me seeing stars. The blood came instantly and the searing pain spread through my entire face. Now I was alternating between icing it and squinting my eyes to watch TV. The doctor determined I didn't have a concussion either, so that was a relief. I'd just be walking around with a banged-up face for a little bit.

As I picked up my remote to flip through the channels, there was a soft beep followed by a click that came from my hotel door. My heart picked up its pace in my chest as the door slowly opened. My room was dark, as it was already nearing eleven o'clock and only the glow from the TV was lighting up the room. I made out the silhouette of his body as he pushed the door shut behind him.

His strides were long and rushed and it didn't take Nico long to close the distance between us. He was still wearing his suit from the game, like he hadn't even bothered going back to his room to change into something more comfortable. He dropped down on the bed beside me, worry laced in his bright blue irises as he gently cupped the sides of my face.

Nico was so tender as his eyes scanned my face before landing on my eyes. "Harper..." His voice cracked around my name. "How bad does it hurt?"

I gave him a small smile. "Probably not as bad as Connor's face."

I saw what Nico did to him after I got hit with my camera. He didn't waste any time before checking him into the boards. It was an aggressive, dirty hit but there was something about the way he reacted that had me melting into a puddle. He came to my defense and knocked Connor out with one hit.

Violence wasn't something I condoned, but seeing someone defend you like that had a way of making you see things differently.

"How bad is the pain, love? Have you taken anything?" He paused for a moment, his eyes desperately searching mine. "Please. What can I do for you?"

His concern shook me straight to my core. "It's not as bad as it looks," I assured him as I motioned to the ice. "I've been icing it, which helps, and I took some ibuprofen."

Nico swallowed roughly, his eyes filled with regret. "I wanted to break through that fucking glass to get to you. I'm sorry it took me so long. I had to stay for the post-game bullshit or I would have been here immediately."

I lifted my hands and slowly pulled his away from my face before lacing our fingers together. "You're here now. That's all that matters."

"I wanted to fucking kill him. I can't believe he pulled something like that."

"It doesn't matter now," I told him, squeezing his hands. "It's over now. You took care of things and that was enough. Neither of us need you in jail and you can't afford to jeopardize your career."

Nico stared at me for a moment as waves of emotion crashed against the shores in his ocean eyes. "I can't stand the thought of anything happening to you, Harper. You're too important to me."

I fell silent as Nico released my hands and rose to his feet beside the bed. My heart crawled into my throat as I watched him strip down to his boxers. "What are you doing?"

"Shh," he murmured softly as he grabbed my arm and pulled me toward the top of the bed and moved the covers away. "I'm not here for anything but to be close to you. I need to feel you in my arms tonight."

"You can't sleep in here," I told him as he laid down on the bed and pulled me into his arms. "Someone will catch us if they see you leaving my room in the morning."

He reached past me, pulling the blankets up over both of us. "I already planned on leaving before everyone else wakes up. Don't make me leave, love. Please just let me be here with you."

There was no possible way I could deny him. Not with the way he was asking me. Not with the way he rushed to my room as soon as he was able to. We were both forming an attachment when there were never supposed to be strings. It was far too late to go back now and that scared me more than anything.

The thought of getting closer to Nico Cirone scared me more than the thought of losing my job. If there was one person in this world who had the power to destroy me, it was him. It wasn't my ex, who may have hurt me physically. It was the person who held my heart, but I was terrified to speak the words out loud.

"I want you to stay," I whispered as he tucked me under his arm and I rested my cheek against his chest.

Nico turned his head and his lips were soft as he pressed them against my forehead. "I'm so sorry he hurt you, love. Fuck. I can't get it out of my head."

"I'm okay, Nico. I promise." I circled my arm around his waist and pulled myself flush against him. I fell silent for a moment, listening to the sound of his heart beating in his chest. "You're all I need. You make everything better."

He was quiet and his fingers were soft as he gently stroked the length of my arm. "I don't know what you're doing to me, Harper, but I don't want you to stop. I don't want whatever this is between us to end."

His words caught me by surprise and I couldn't help the words that escaped me next. "I don't want this to end either."

"And you still don't want a label?" His voice was soft and tender.

I shook my head against him. "We can't. Not with the way things are."

"I won't wait forever, love." A declaration. "I'll give you the time to let this be what it is, but you're already mine. If you take too long, I'll be the one to slap a label on it without any more hesitation."

"I want to be with you, Nico. You weren't a part of my plan when I moved here, but I can't get away from you and I don't want to." I fell silent as I collected my thoughts and chose my next words carefully. "Putting a label on it makes it real."

He rested his chin against the top of my head as he held me tightly. "And you don't want it to be real."

I shook my head. "That's the problem… I do want it to be real."

"You're contradicting yourself, Harper."

I lifted my head and turned my body to look at him. "I want it to be real, but I'm terrified of what will happen. Look at my last relationship."

Nico scowled. "I am nothing like him." He stared directly into my soul. "I am not him, Harper. I will never, ever fucking hurt you."

I swallowed over the emotion that was thick in my throat. "I know, you're the complete opposite of him. You make me feel things I've never felt before and I'm not afraid that you'll hurt me the same way he did."

"So, what are you afraid of?"

I stared back at him. "What happens when you grow tired of me? When you decide you want something else or someone different?" I raked my teeth over my bottom lip. "I don't know that I would survive the ways you could destroy me."

Nico's eyes pierced mine. "You are it for me, Harper.

You are everything. I don't give a fuck about anyone else. And growing tired of you is impossible. If anything, I will always want more of you."

"You can say that, but there's no way for you to guarantee it."

"Then let me show you, Harper," he said softly as he stroked the side of my face. "Take a chance and fall with me."

"You say it like it's so simple."

He smirked. "Because it is, love. I know you've been hurt in the past and it's hard for you to trust. All I'm asking for is a chance to show you that I mean every fucking word I say to you."

"Okay," I whispered as my heart pounded erratically against my rib cage. I slowly lowered my head back to his chest and listened to the thrumming sound underneath.

"Thank you," he whispered into my hair as he held me close again.

We both fell silent for a moment, lost in our own thoughts, but he was consuming mine. He plagued my mind, but in the best way possible. I wanted to believe him, I wanted to trust him. I wanted to fall with him so he could catch me before I crashed into the ground. There was a hesitation on my end and I knew it was because of my ex, along with the fact that we were breaking the rules of the organization we both worked for.

"We were never supposed to get in this deep," I murmured against his bare chest as I ran my hand across his chiseled torso.

Nico chuckled lightly as he traced invisible patterns along my back.

"Too late, love," he said as he pressed his lips to my forehead once more. "We're already in deep and there's no way out now."

He was right.

I could feel myself sinking deeper into the depths of Nico Cirone and I wasn't sure that I ever wanted to come up for air again.

Chapter Twenty

Nico

Our flight left early the next morning and I made sure I was back in my room before everyone else was up. Wes didn't even stir when I snuck in and got into my bed. I laid there, still thinking about her as Wes's alarm went off. Those damn bruises on her face—I fucking hated them. I wanted to wash them all away.

I wanted to take her pain and give it all to him, but I couldn't. She was right. It was over and I had to let it go… for now, until I saw him on the ice again.

We all boarded onto the jet and flew back to the city with the weight of our loss hanging heavily over our heads. Our coach wasn't particularly thrilled about it and he wanted us on the ice as soon as we touched down in Orchid Beach.

I didn't even get to say anything to Harper because she disappeared as soon as we got off the jet. Wes and I both walked to our cars in silence before heading back to the training facility. It was a brutal practice, one that

189

we had to do without pucks. Those were always the worst and as if we didn't work our asses off last night... we were all fucking exhausted after practice.

As I sat in the locker room after getting a shower, I pulled out my phone and sent Harper a message. I was able to clear my mind while out on the ice because of the intensity of the drills we were forced to do, but as soon as I was back in the locker room, I couldn't help myself as my thoughts drifting back to her.

NICO

Did you get home all right? I didn't even see you leave.

She responded almost instantly, sending me a selfie of her lying on her couch. My eyebrows pinched together in disapproval as I saw the bruises that were deepening in color under her eyes. The tip of her nose was scraped from the camera and my jaw clenched.

HARPER

I did. I was exhausted after traveling and haven't left my couch since.

NICO

Good. You need to rest. Call me later?

Wes walked over to me and stopped in front of me. His hair was damp from his shower and he was wearing a sweat suit. "You want to hang out?"

My phone vibrated in my hand and I looked up at my friend. "Come over if you want. I planned on just lying around."

"You're not going to go see her?"

I shook my head, as I quickly read her message. "I'm pretty sure she just wants to lay low and I don't want to overstep at all."

HARPER

I'm going to take a nap, but I'll call you later this evening.

Wes nodded with a look of approval. "Probably a good idea. You don't want to scare her away with your obsessiveness."

I cut my eyes at him. "I am not obsessive."

Wes snorted. "Dude... you know what—I'm not even going to argue with you. If you can't see your obsession with her, then you have some serious issues."

I laughed as I shook my head at him as everyone began to clear out of the locker room. "You know I would never admit something like that."

"Smart of you not to," he agreed with a smirk. "Although, I'm not stupid. I see shit."

"I'm sure you do," I told him as I grabbed my stuff. "Meet me over at my place. We can play Call of Duty or something."

"Deal."

———

Wes and I were both sitting on my couch, each of us drinking a beer while we waited for our pizza to be delivered. We were playing video games, just talking about mindless shit. We went over the shit show of our game until it started to shift into a territory that I wasn't sure I wanted to talk to him about.

"So, things are getting pretty serious between the two of you?"

I lifted my beer to my mouth and took a swig as we waited to join another match on Call of Duty. "Yeah, and I don't know what to do about it."

Wes glanced over at me as he leaned forward to be closer to the TV. "What do you mean? I mean, I know shit between the two of you is different since there's a lot at stake with her job and everything."

"I tried to get her to quit. I told her to just move in with me and let me take care of her."

A string of laughter escaped Wes as he threw his head backward. He leaned against the back of the couch just as the game started and he instantly got shot. "Fuck," he grumbled as he sat upright again. His focus was on the game, but he wasn't going to let the conversation go. "Bro. You're such a liar saying that you aren't obsessed with her. I'm assuming she declined your proposition?"

"Oh, of course," I told him with a laugh. "I didn't think she would actually agree. She's too independent to do something like that, but I figured it was worth a shot. She's been working on shooting weddings and other things to try and get away from sports. Her dream is to have her own business doing that kind of stuff instead."

Wes was silent for a moment. "You want my honest opinion?"

I stared at the TV as I ducked around some objects in

the game. "No, but I'm thinking you're going to give it to me anyways."

"I think you need to tell her how you really feel. You know how short life is and I don't know what the hell you're waiting for anymore."

Our round ended and I looked over at him just as the bell rang. "I did tell her how I feel." I rose to my feet and grabbed my wallet before disappearing from my apartment to go get our pizza from the lobby. As I reached my floor again and brought the box back into the living room, Wes took a sip of his beer and stared at me.

"Did you tell her that you're in love with her?"

I froze in place just as I flipped open the pizza box. "What? No. Why the fuck would I do that?"

"Because that's how you really feel," he said matter-of-factly while he grabbed a piece of pizza. "You're only lying to yourself if you think you're not in love with her."

The heaviness of his words settled in my bones and I sat there for a moment as I stared at the TV. My eyes weren't focused on what was happening on the screen as my mind ran wild with possibilities. I swallowed hard over the lump that had lodged itself in my throat. Were my feelings for her that obvious?

"Don't worry," Wes cut through my thoughts as he chewed a mouthful of pizza. "I won't tell anyone your secret. I'm like a vault."

I let out an exasperated sigh as I finally grabbed a slice for myself. "Am I that obvious?"

Wes shrugged. "Nah, not really. I just know you well enough that I can tell."

"I can't tell her."

His brow furrowed. "Why not?"

"Because I don't want to complicate things any more than I already have. It will only make things messier."

Wes took another sip of his beer. "I don't know, bro. Things are always complicated. There's nothing you can do to change it, but I think it's worth telling her." He set his beer down on the coffee table. "You might be surprised when you find out she feels the same way."

"How could you possibly know that?" I questioned him as I sank back into the couch.

"If you can't tell then you really are in fucking denial," Wes told me as he rolled his eyes. "She looks at you like you're the only thing that matters, Nico. I think you'll be surprised when you finally tell her how you feel."

I mulled over his words as I sipped on my beer. Wes directed his attention away from me as he typed something out on his phone. My mind drifted to my mother and how quickly she slipped away from us. Life was unpredictable. Things could change in the blink of an eye. Wes was right. I needed to come clean with Harper and tell her how I actually felt about her, but it terrified me.

There was something about being that vulnerable with someone that was frightening. She already had the power to destroy me, she just didn't know it yet.

From the moment I met Harper Jensen, I knew I needed to make her mine. Even after that night at the club, something about her had struck something deep inside me. I couldn't get her out of my head, and then it was as if the universe heard my thoughts and brought her back into my life.

I wasn't looking for a relationship when I met her. What happened between us was just supposed to be something fun. She was a good luck charm that I knew I couldn't lose; she was just looking for an escape. Our arrangement was supposed to serve two simple purposes. But things between us shifted into something more.

Harper was under my skin, she was in my heart and in my soul. I wanted her to be a permanent fixture in my life. I wanted to savor the moments between us and never let them go.

"I hate to be the one who eats and runs, but I'm going to head out."

I looked back at Wes who was already standing up from the couch. "Since when do you have plans that I don't know about?"

He glanced at me with a look of guilt in his eyes, almost as if he got caught doing something. "Who said I have any plans?"

I scowled at him. "You're abruptly leaving to go home and hang out by yourself?"

A chuckle escaped him. "Touché." He paused for a second as mischief danced in his irises. "I'm just going to go help a friend out with some research stuff."

"You have other friends?"

Wes gave me the middle finger. "You're a dick."

I stared at him as I raised a suspicious eyebrow.

"How do you know all my secrets, but I don't know yours?"

Wes gave me a crooked grin. "Because I'm the vault, not you."

"Please tell me it's not Harper's friend, Ava."

"What?" His brow furrowed. "Absolutely not. I promise it's no one you know. It's just this girl I met and I promised I'd help her with some research for the books she's writing—"

I held my hands up to stop him. "Forget I asked," I laughed as I shook my head. "I don't even want to know about the shit you've gotten yourself into."

Wes laughed along with me as he headed toward the elevator door. "I'm not quite sure what I've even gotten myself into, but I'm along for the ride now. Wish me luck!"

"Good luck?" I spoke the words half in question, half in declaration as I heard the elevator doors open. He stepped inside and they quickly closed behind him before he began his descent down to the lobby.

Wes was definitely more of a free spirit than anyone else, so I wasn't really surprised by his new adventure. It sounded pretty on-brand for him. It made sense why he was reading romance books on the plane now. I wondered if he was reading her books. I didn't need to wonder about what kind of research he'd be helping her with.

As I began to clean up the pizza and the empty beer bottles, my mind drifted back to Harper. I needed to be honest with her. I had given her the watered-down version of my feelings, and she deserved to know the truth. Being so open and vulnerable with someone wasn't the only thing that scared me about it. I was afraid I would scare her away too, and that was the last thing I wanted to do.

She deserved to know and I knew I had to tell her. It wasn't something I could just do over the phone. I needed to tell her in person and just prepare myself for the possibility of sending her running in the opposite direction.

All I could do was hope for the best.

And hope she felt the same way I did.

Chapter Twenty-one

Harper

As I stood in the bathroom, I tried to apply makeup to the bruise across the bridge of my nose and the ones that settled beneath my eyes. There was only so much I could apply before it was noticeable that I was just caking it on.

Nico texted me this morning and asked if I wanted to go get lunch with him. They had a home game tonight and then he'd be back on the road for about a week-long stretch for away games. I told Nico I needed to go see about getting a new camera lens and he was more than happy to offer to take me to the store.

I had meant to do it as soon as we got back from Vegas but I had spent the past two days fighting off gnarly headaches from the swelling in my face. Today was the first day I felt a little bit better and a little more like myself. I was surprised the pain had gotten worse than when it initially happened.

My phone vibrated from the counter as I applied my

mascara and was finishing up my makeup routine. I gave myself a last glance in the mirror and shrugged. It wasn't the best but it would do.

NICO

I'm outside. Did you want me to come up?

HARPER

I'll be right down.

I flicked off the bathroom light, grabbed my keys and purse, and slid my feet into a pair of sneakers before heading down to Nico. His sleek car was parked along the curb outside of my apartment building and he was leaning against the side of it with his hands tucked in the front pockets of his gray joggers.

A smile crept onto his lips as his gaze collided with mine. "Hey you."

My mouth went dry at the sight of him and my heart pounded to its own beat in my chest. There was nothing rhythmic about it. "Hey," I murmured and smiled back at him as he pushed off the car and opened the door for me.

I sat down and he waited patiently before shutting it behind me. I watched him circle around the front of the car before sliding into his seat. He slid his hand into mine before pulling the car away from the curb. He took us to a small coffee shop not far into the city. It was about two blocks away from the camera store.

"If I park here, would you want to just walk?" he inquired as he found a spot in one of the parking garages. "I needed to stop to get a new dress shirt and there's a store on our walk."

"That's perfect with me," I told him as he pulled into the parking spot and turned off the engine. He hopped out of the car in a rush while I was still getting my stuff together and he met me at my door as he pulled it open for me.

I smiled up at him and he took my camera bag from me. He slid it over his shoulder and his hand found mine once again before we headed out of the garage and to the coffee shop. Nico's steps were light, almost as if he were floating. There was never a nervousness to him. If there was anyone who oozed confidence and was sure of themselves, it was him.

His energy was contagious. He wasn't arrogant, he wasn't cocky. He was simply just confident in the things he knew and believed in.

It didn't take us long to eat our sandwiches at the coffee shop and we were heading down the street, walking past shops as we made our way to the camera store first. Nico carried my bag and held my hand until we reached the front door. He paused to open it for me and let me walk in ahead of him.

As we stepped inside, I was captivated by the different displays set up throughout the store. There were various cameras and styles, along with different lenses, attachments, and accessories. I turned to Nico and attempted to take the camera bag from him.

"I need to see if they have one similar to the one that was broken," I explained to him as he ducked his shoulder and dodged my reach. "Can I have my bag, please?"

His lips stretched into a grin and he shook his head at me. "I'm sorry, love. I can't do that."

My eyebrows pinched together in confusion. "Why not? I need to show them the broken lens."

Nico shook his head again. "We're not here to get you a new lens."

"Yes, we are," I reminded him as confusion set within my expression.

His eyes were bright and his lips parted. "Pick out a new camera, love. Whatever you want and whatever you need to go with it."

My eyes widened and I quickly shook my head. "You don't have to do that, Nico. It's too expensive. Plus, the camera I have is fine. I don't need something new."

"Let me do this for you, Harper," he said softly as he raised his hand to cup the side of my face. "I want you to pick out whatever you want—the price doesn't matter."

His words had me staring back at him in shock. The caliber of camera that I had to use for the shoots I did was very pricey. I didn't think Nico knew what he was really saying by telling me to pick out whatever, regardless of the cost.

"I can't let you do that," I retorted, my voice barely audible as his eyes stared into mine.

"I'm not asking you to," he countered, still cupping my cheek. "I want to do this for you and if you don't pick out what you want, then I'm going to end up picking out something that will most likely be the wrong thing."

"Nico…" My voice trailed off as I swallowed over the emotion that was thick in my throat. No one had ever done something like this for me before. It had nothing to do with the money, but more of the meaning and principal behind it.

His lips were soft as he pressed them against mine. "Come on, love. Let's get whatever it is you need."

There was no argument with Nico when he was insisting on something. He made it clear from the start that he gets what he wants and he was making sure that I reaped the same benefits. When I picked out a camera and was mindful of the price, he made sure they gave me the fully loaded, more expensive model instead.

I had no idea how much money was spent in that store and I wasn't going to be the one who asked him or fought him on it. It was hard letting someone do something like that for me but when I saw the joy on Nico's face, I knew it was worth it. He had quite a few different love languages and I was learning that giving was one of them.

As we walked down the street, Nico's fingers were laced through mine. He was silent with a thoughtful look on his face as we moved side by side. We passed by the store he had said he wanted to stop at, yet he didn't stop. His footsteps weren't rushed, yet he walked right by it.

I came to a stop and he glanced down at me as he stopped beside me. "What's wrong?"

He didn't seem to have any idea and I angled my

head to the side as I looked up at him. "You didn't need to get a dress shirt, did you?"

Nico smiled and shook his head. "I just wanted the chance to hold your hand for a little while longer. For us to be out like this without anyone knowing anything about either of us." He paused for a moment as he raked his teeth over his bottom lip. "It's almost like we're free to be together here."

My heart crawled into my throat as he turned to face me. People moved past us on the sidewalk but neither of us paid them any mind. They didn't exist. It was just the two of us as the world stopped spinning. His fingers were soft as he brushed the hair from my face and tucked the strands behind my ears.

"I need to tell you something," he said softly, his voice tentative and hoarse with emotion. His eyes searched mine and he folded his lips between his teeth.

I swallowed and nodded. "Okay…"

His chest rose as he sucked in a deep breath. "I'm in love with you, Harper," he said slowly as he exhaled. "You're all I think about, day and night. You're the only person I want to spend my time with. I tried to fight it, but I can't anymore. I can't keep up this charade. I love you."

My eyes widened as I stared back at him. His words slid across my eardrums and seeped into my veins. My heart picked up its pace as it began to race in my chest and I was lost in the depths of his ocean eyes.

He was never supposed to love me, but we didn't have a say when it came to love. It made its own rules and we had to play by them. Neither of our hearts ever stood a chance and he was spreading through my system like an addiction I never wanted to recover from.

My lips parted and a ragged breath escaped me as Nico smiled the smile that was only reserved for me. "You don't have to say anything, love," he assured me as he pressed his lips to my forehead. "I just need you to know my feelings for you and the intensity behind them."

I wanted to say it back to him, but I found myself struggling to form the words. If I spoke it out loud, then that made it true. And if my feelings were true, that made whatever this was between us real. And if it were real then he would have the power to break my heart.

Who was I kidding?

He has had the power.

"I love you too, Nico," I admitted softly as I reached into my own chest and pulled out my own heart as I handed it over to him. "I've been in love with you longer than I've wanted to admit because it scares me more than anything."

"I know you've been hurt in the past, Harper," he said with hesitation as his eyes searched mine. "I can promise you I'll never hurt you."

I stared back at him. "That's the thing... the way he hurt me comes nowhere close to what you could do to me." I let out the breath I didn't know I was holding. "You would ruin me completely."

His face dipped down to mine. "Never, Harper. You're it for me."

He sealed his promise with a kiss as his lips melted

into mine. He was tender and attentive as he stole the air from my lungs and I willingly let him.

Nico could take whatever he wanted from me until there was nothing left.

Chapter Twenty-Two

Nico

As much as I loved traveling, I was tired of doing it without Harper. It was getting old having to travel to different cities and leaving her behind. With her job, it wasn't guaranteed that she would be sent along as the photographer for the game. It seemed like they rotated through their people and her time would be coming again soon, but not soon enough.

Instead, I was stuck on the road for a week without her and I was a fiend for her like an addict looking for their next fix. I was tired of only being able to see her face through the screen on my phone. It just wasn't cutting it anymore. I needed to feel her skin beneath my fingertips. I wanted her voice in my ears as she surrounded and consumed me.

She had her first newborn shoot while I was away and the excitement that lit up her face when we talked was contagious. She and Ava went out to get different props and things she would need at her client's home where she did the shoot.

I wanted to buy her a fucking building with her own office. One where she could open up her own studio. Getting her to allow me to buy her a damn camera was a feat in itself. I would have to take baby steps and work up to getting Harper her own studio. Harper wasn't exactly one who liked to let others try and take care of her.

I pulled up out in front of her apartment building and sent her a text to let her know I was there. I got out of my car and stood by the side as I waited for her. It didn't take her long to come down and a smile danced across my lips as I saw my girl.

We were caught in a weird place. We both admitted our feelings for one another, yet there was no real definition between us. A part of me cared while the other part of me didn't give two shits. At the end of the day, she was my girl and that was all that fucking mattered.

"There you are." I smiled as I stepped away from my car and met her by the door. Instead of pulling it open for her, I pulled her flush against me.

She looked up at me, her eyes dancing under the moonlight. "I missed you," she breathed.

"Not as much as I missed you," I countered as I swiftly claimed her mouth with mine. It was a hasty kiss, but I couldn't wait to taste her. She was mine and I planned on reminding her of that every time I saw her.

"Come on," I told her as I broke apart from her and ushered her to the car as I opened the door for her. "I made reservations and I don't want us to be late." I paused for a moment as I leaned down to look at her with a devious smirk pulling on my lips. "That is, unless you wanted to skip out on dinner completely and do something else instead…"

Harper laughed softly and shook her head as she pulled the seat belt across her body. "Let's eat first. We have a history of not eating if we tend to other needs first."

I smiled down at her, my laugh matching hers as I pushed the door shut. She wasn't wrong there. Although, I would much rather eat her than dinner right now.

I took her back to Dare and I watched the excitement in her eyes as we were seated at another private booth. The last time we were here, things got heated pretty quickly and we ended up taking our food to go. Tonight I wanted to do things a little differently. If she was going to make me wait, then I wasn't going to make it easy for her at all.

We were seated with our drinks, and our food was already ordered, as I sat next to her with my hand on her thigh. "I had some other ideas for what we could do tonight, but I wasn't sure if you would be interested or not…"

Harper raised an eyebrow. "What did you have in mind?"

I slowly moved my hand between her thighs and gripped her flesh. "I want to take you ice skating."

"Umm…" Harper paused as a nervous laugh fell from her lips. "So, I'm embarrassed to say this since you do it for a living, but I've never ice-skated before."

A smile pulled on my lips and lifted them upward. "I was honestly hoping you would say that."

"Why's that?" she said with a curious look in her eyes as she tilted her head to the side.

"Because I want as many of your firsts that I can have."

Her tongue darted out to wet her lips and I watched a wave of emotion pass through her bright blue irises. She ducked her gaze down to the table as she lifted her drink. I watched the hues of pink appear on her cheeks and I couldn't help but feel satisfied.

"Where were we going to go?"

I winked. "I think I might know of a place."

As we stood outside of the stadium, Harper glared at me. "You want to break in? Do you want us to get arrested?"

I laughed as I looked over at her as we reached the players' entrance. My hand dipped into my pocket and I pulled out a key. "It's technically not breaking in if you have a key, right?"

She didn't look amused. "Nico... if anyone catches us here, we're fucked."

I swiftly pulled her flush against me and dipped my face down to hers as I nipped at her bottom lip. "This is what you're worried about getting caught doing with me?" I laughed quietly as I pulled her bottom lip between my teeth. "I think there are worse things we could get caught doing."

"Nico..." She said my name in a warning tone, yet her voice was hoarse and thick with lust.

Releasing her from my grip, I stepped away from her as I slid the key into the lock and opened the door. I looked back at Harper who was standing behind me with her arms crossed over her chest. "Are you coming with me or are you going to play it safe instead?"

Conflict washed over her expression and finally she sighed and took a step after me. "If we get caught, this is your fault."

"I'll gladly take all the blame, love." I laughed again as I pulled her into the stadium with me. Whether we got caught in here or for doing something else together, protecting Harper was my number one concern. If there was one of us that would take the fall, I would do everything I possibly could to make it be me and not her.

It was quiet as we walked through the concrete halls. There was no one here but us and it was the first time I had ever experienced this before. When I was in high school, we used to sneak into one of the local rinks to play pickup games in the middle of the night. It happened a few times before we got caught, but then the owner just started leaving the door unlocked for us instead.

There were soft lights glowing throughout the building, probably for actual security if and when they patrolled the area. It was just enough light to guide us to the locker room and I pulled Harper inside. The room was dark and I flicked on the light as it illuminated the entire room. Harper walked over and sat down on the bench as she looked up at me.

She sat right by my name and I couldn't help but

smile down at her. "Do you even have skates I can wear?"

Shit.

"I was thinking you could probably just wear Wes's or something. They're not going to fit but I'll tie them tight enough that it shouldn't matter."

She continued to look at me, unconvinced, but shrugged instead. I walked over to grab Wes's skates as she kicked off her sneakers. I moved back in front of her and slid each of her feet into the skates before lacing them up. She was quiet and watched me as I tied them tightly and set them back on the floor.

I grabbed my own skates and put them on before helping her up to her feet. She was a little wobbly and I held my arm out for her to hold on to for support.

"This feels like a terrible idea," she muttered as I began to lead her down the tunnel toward the ice. "I'm going to break my ankle or something."

I chuckled and shook my head at her dramatics. "Are your skates not tight enough?"

"Well, considering the fact that it feels like there's no blood flowing to my feet... I think they're tight enough."

"Then your ankles should be safe," I told her as I led her onto the bench and opened up the door. "Come with me, love," I said softly as I stepped out onto the ice and turned around to face her with my hand out. "I won't let you fall."

Harper hesitated for a moment before sliding her hand into mine. I helped her onto the ice and her eyes were wide as her feet slid involuntarily. I laughed and held her steady as she attempted to get her bearings. One of her hands were in mine and the other was clutching my arm as she held on for her life.

"This feels so unnatural," she breathed and shook her head. "You guys make it look so easy."

I slowly began to move and pulled her along with me. She slowly released her grip on my arm and I watched her as she watched my feet move. She tried to mimic the movements as we moved around the ice. "See, you're getting it. Just move your feet like this," I told her as I alternated between pushing off on one foot and switching to the opposite.

Harper tried to do what I was doing and her foot slid a little farther than she wanted. A nervous laugh escaped her as she clutched on to me again. "Nope, not doing that," she said as she shuffled along. "I'm good doing whatever this is."

We did one lap around the arena and as we made our way back toward the bench, I saw a light flash on in the other locker room. There was movement in the room and I caught a glimpse of someone moving down the tunnel. My heart stopped in my chest and I quickly pulled her to me.

"Fuck," I muttered as I lifted her up in my arms and skated faster to get off the ice. "We gotta go, Harper."

"What's wrong?" Her voice shook with concern. I pulled her through the door and broke off into a jog as I led her down the tunnel with me. We stepped back into the locker room and I left the light off as I pushed her against the wall and shielded her with my own body.

"Shh," I murmured as I gently pressed my finger

against her lips. "I saw the security guard walking toward the ice down the other tunnel."

"You're kidding, right?"

I shook my head even though she couldn't see the movement through the darkness. My heart pounded erratically and I couldn't get it to slow down. "I wish I was."

The footsteps outside the room got louder and Harper's body grew rigid against mine. I sucked in a deep breath and held it as the door slowly opened. As it opened, we were carefully tucked just behind one of the cabinets so the guard didn't see either of us as he flicked on the lights.

Harper's eyes were wide as she stared up at me. I moved my hand over her mouth, covering it completely as I shook my head. I didn't want either of us to get caught and the adrenaline was surging through my system right now.

The security guard let out a sigh and the light flickered back off before the door closed behind him. I waited three more seconds before finally exhaling the breath I was holding in. I removed my hand from Harper's mouth and she exhaled simultaneously. The darkness had surrounded us again and I couldn't see Harper, but I could feel her under the palms of my hands as she was pressed against me.

Her chest rose and fell in rapid succession and I slid my hands along her torso, using all of my senses but sight to absorb her. "What are you doing, Nico?" she questioned me breathlessly.

"There's no way we can go back out there now

without getting caught," I murmured as I slid my hands up over her shoulders and pushed her coat away from her body. "We have to wait it out now until he goes away."

"You really didn't think this through, did you?"

I stifled a laugh and shook my head. "I thought we would be good and be able to have time to skate before anyone showed up. Looks like plans have changed."

"Now what?" she asked me.

I smiled as I slid my hands under the bottom hem of her shirt. "We can go to one of the public rinks and do their public skates instead."

Harper was silent for a moment. "You mean that was always an option? You just decided you wanted to do something illegal instead for my first time?"

"What's life if you're not taking risks?" My face dipped down to hers. "I'm willing to risk it all for you, love. What about you?"

She slid her arms up around the back of my neck and pulled me closer until her lips brushed against mine.

"I'm here, aren't I?"

My lips collided with hers as I staked my claim on what was already mine.

She was mine and she was willing to risk it all for us.

Chapter Twenty-three

Harper

The room was dark and I couldn't see Nico but I could feel him. My senses were heightened and his palms were soft against my skin as he lifted my shirt up over my head. The air in the room was cold against my skin and a shiver slid up my spine as it was a contrast to the warmth that was rapidly spreading through my body.

"I can't see anything, Nico," I said as he moved his lips to the side of my neck and was sliding his fingers under the waistband of my leggings. I was pushing his shirt up his torso and we broke apart as he pulled it up over his head and tossed it onto the floor.

His hands were back on my skin, warming me with his touch. "You don't need to see, love," he breathed as his lips captured mine once again. "Just feel."

He slowly inched his way down my body, bending his knees as he pulled my leggings down to my ankles. He cursed under his breath as he reached the ice skates that were still on my feet. I didn't know how he did it so quickly in the dark, but in less than a minute he had them untied and was throwing them over in the opposite direction.

They clattered into something, making more noise than either of us had intended. I jumped at the sound, a gasp escaping me simultaneously.

"Shh, love," Nico said softly as he ran his hands up my bare thighs. He had me stripped naked with the cool air surrounding us but my body was on fire. "We don't want anyone to hear us."

"You're the one making all the noise," I reminded him as he slid his hand underneath my thigh. He lifted it into the air before hooking it over his shoulder.

"That doesn't compare to how loud I could make you be." Nico's face dipped between my legs and I felt his breath against my pussy as he exhaled. "I need you to be quiet for me, baby. Can you do that while I eat this sweet pussy?"

I swallowed roughly and nodded even though he couldn't see me. He ran his tongue along my center, circling once around my clit before he pulled his mouth away from me. My hands were in his hair, laced through his tousled waves. "Why'd you stop?"

"I need your words, Harper. Are you going to be a good girl and be fucking quiet while I make you come?"

"Yes," I breathed, my voice half catching in my throat as I tightened my grip on his hair.

Nico chuckled softly before bringing his lips back to my core. He moved his tongue with precision and skill as he ate me like I was his last meal. He was sucking, tasting, licking, and driving me fucking insane all at once. My mind could barely keep up with the different movements and the pleasure was already building inside me.

He settled on my clit, running his tongue over it again and again, applying various degrees of pressure. He repeated the movement, flicking his tongue faster, and he was driving me closer and closer to the edge. My teeth were cutting into the flesh of my bottom lip as I bit down to refrain from moaning.

My hands were still in his hair. His hands were gripping my thighs as he spread them wider to lick me again. My head was swimming and he wasn't showing any signs of stopping anytime soon. He slid one hand along the inside of my leg before he was pushing a finger inside of me. He slowly began to move it in and out before adding another digit.

It was almost too much as he was driving me absolutely fucking insane. His fingers pumped harder in and out of me and his tongue was still on my clit. He was fucking me with his mouth and hand at the same time and Jesus Christ... he was a force to be reckoned with. Nico knew exactly what he was doing and I had no complaints whatsoever.

I was seeing stars. The warmth was quickly spreading through my system and Nico was on a mission to steal the pleasure straight from my body. He began to curl his fingers as he massaged my insides. As he pressed against the soft spot inside while still working his tongue, it wasn't long before I was close to losing myself.

My legs were clamping around his head and he fought against me, holding them open as he fucked me relentlessly with his mouth. My hips bucked as my orgasm tore through my body and it took everything in me not to cry out in pleasure. He didn't move his mouth away as he drank from me, lapping at my pussy until there was nothing left.

My entire body felt like it was going to float through the ceiling and I couldn't focus on anything at the moment. Nico slid his hand under my other thigh and lifted me into the air as he stood upright. I liked his hands on me. It gave me a sense of security, like I knew where he was, even though I may not have known what his next move was going to be.

Nico lifted me away from the side of the cabinet and walked deeper into the dark room. My legs were around his waist and I held on to him.

"How can you see where you're going?" I whispered in his ear as I wrapped my arms around the back of his neck.

"I can't, but I know this room like the back of my hand."

He paused as he kicked his foot out and felt around. Holding me against him with one arm, he reached down and felt around until he must have found what he was looking for. His hands were back on my hips and he slowly began to lower me onto one of the benches.

My legs fell away from his waist and he pulled my arms loose as he stood upright for a moment. I heard the sound of his clothing as he lowered his pants and boxers to the top of his skates and was back between my legs in a fraction of a second. The tip of his cock pressed against my pussy and he slowly eased into me with one fluid movement.

The air escaped me in a rush and he was hovering above me with his hand planted on the bench above my head. It was an awkward position as he tried to move with nothing to really lean against. I blocked him with the muscles of the insides of my thighs.

"What's wrong, love?" He lowered his face to mine and nipped at my bottom lip.

I planted my hands on his chest and pushed him away. "I want to be on top."

He fell silent for a moment. "You want to fuck me, Harper?" His voice was hoarse and thick with need.

Nico moved away, pulling out of me as he stood back up. I slowly sat up before climbing off the bench. I couldn't see anything and put my hands out to feel for him as he laid back on the bench. His legs were off the bench with his knees bent and his feet planted on the floor. I found his waist with my fingers and I lifted my leg to straddle him.

Taking his cock in my hand, I positioned it against my pussy and slowly lowered myself down onto him. Nico sucked in a sharp breath as I slid down, taking his entire length inside of me until he was filling me to the brim.

"Goddamn, Harper," he groaned as his hands found my hips. "This pussy was made for me and only me."

"I belong to you, Nico," I told him as I began to move my hips, shifting my weight as I slid up and down the length of his cock. "You make me feel like no one else ever has."

"And no one will ever make you feel the way I do," he assured me as his fingers dug into my flesh. "Now, be quiet and ride my cock like a good girl."

Lifting myself up again, I planted my hands on his chest as I began to bounce up and down harder. He was taking some of the work from me as he topped me from the bottom and thrust into me at the same time. We were both moving together, each of us fucking the other to our own perfect melody.

"So fucking good," he growled as he thrust his hips up harder. He snaked an arm around my back and pulled my body down to his in a rush. We were chest to chest and I buried my face in his neck as he took over completely.

He was in control, holding me in place with one arm while gripping my ass with his other hand. His hips were lifting off the bench over and over as he fucked me harder with each thrust. He was pounding into me with such an urgent need. I could feel my own orgasm beginning to build within me again and he wasn't far behind me.

"Don't make a fucking sound," he growled in my ear as he slammed into me again. "Bite my shoulder if you have to, but I don't want to hear a fucking sound from you while I make you come."

Nico didn't stop as he fucked me harder. There was no way to hide the sounds of our bodies moving together and our panted breathing filling the room. Nico slid his hand up to my nape, keeping my face buried in his neck as my orgasm began to build. It was coming on strong and I couldn't stop it from happening any longer.

It tore through my body like an earthquake as I shattered around him. My teeth bit into his flesh as I clamped down to keep myself from crying out from the pleasure that was consuming my entire being. Nico rocked up into me once more before he was losing himself, filling me with his cum. His warmth spread inside me and he was in my veins, running rampant as he continued to fuck my system with the ecstasy that was taking over every one of my senses.

I felt like I was never going to come back down to solid ground after this.

"Fuck," Nico murmured, as he held me on top of him. I slowly sat up, feeling the ache in my bones from him fucking me like he did. There was nothing bad about the ache. It was the exact kind I lived for from him. "You're absolutely perfect, Harper. I don't know what I did in life to deserve you."

I stared down at him in the dark, even though I couldn't see him, and felt along the side of his face instead. "I know exactly what you did. It's that big, loving heart of yours."

We were both a mess as we tried to catch our breaths. My legs felt like Jell O as I climbed off of him. His cum was sliding down the insides of my thighs and Nico sat up on the bench, suddenly flashing on a small light. I noticed it was the flashlight from his phone that he found on the floor with his pants.

He flashed the light at me and trailed it down my body

before stopping at my legs. "I love seeing my cum running down your legs. Come here, love," he murmured.

Obeying him, I stepped closer until his hand was sliding along my thigh. He dragged his fingers through his cum, collecting it on his fingertips before he slid them back inside me. My body twitched and he pulled his fingers from me as he slowly stood up.

He pressed his damp, sticky fingertips against my bottom lip. "Open for me, baby. I want you to taste us together."

My lips parted and he slid his fingers inside my mouth. I closed them around him and swirled my tongue around his fingers as I tasted the saltiness of him and the sweetness of my own juices. Nico's eyes were on mine, dark with lust and approval.

"Goddamn, that's so fucking hot," he said with his voice hoarse. "I fucking love you."

A soft laugh escaped me as he pulled his fingers from my mouth. "I love you too," I told him as I looked up at him. "We should probably get out of here before we get caught, though."

"You're right," he said with a smile as he collected his shirt from the floor and pulled up his pants. He flashed the light over to where my clothes were, then he waited patiently while I got dressed and walked over to me. I glanced down at his feet and pointed at his skates.

"Oh shit," he chuckled softly as he shook his head. "I suppose I should take those off too."

He quickly unlaced his skates and put them back where they belonged. I watched him while he picked up Wes's skates and put them in his area too. Nico met me by the door and turned off his flashlight as he pulled open the door to the locker room and looked out into the hallway for anyone.

"Coast is clear," he told me as he held his hand out to me. I slid my fingers through his and he broke out into a jog, pulling me along with him. His stride was much longer than mine but I ran along with him until we were finally outside of the building.

Giggles escaped us like little children from the adrenaline rush we had just experienced running from the stadium. Hell, the entire night was a fucking rush like I had never felt before. Sneaking around like that so we wouldn't get caught. Skating for my first time with him. Having sex in the locker room.

I looked over at him as we sat in his car, getting ready to leave to go back to my place for the night. "Have you ever done that before?"

Nico looked over at me with his eyebrows drawn together. "Done what?"

"All of it," I said in a rush. "Snuck into the stadium to take another girl there to skate and then fucked her in the locker room."

His facial expression relaxed and his mouth twitched as he raised an eyebrow. "Would you be mad if I did?"

Yes. "No."

He smirked. "You're a terrible liar, Harper. But the answer is no. I've never done any of that with anyone but you."

"Good," I told him with a smile as I slid my hand into his. "I want some of your firsts too."

Nico pulled his car from the parking spot as he looked over at me with his ocean eyes.

"I can't promise you all of my firsts, but I can promise you every single one of my lasts."

Chapter Twenty-four

Nico

Harper was still in my room getting dressed when I heard the elevator doors ding and slide open. I started walking toward the doors when my sister stepped into view with her suitcase in tow. She was only here for the weekend, but Giana never traveled lightly.

Her face lit up when she saw me and she ran over, jumping up to give me a hug. She was only two years younger than me, but the size difference was definitely noticeable. Giana stood just below my shoulder and I lifted her up into the air in silence.

As I set her back on her feet, she took a step back and her eyes pierced mine. *"Is she here?"* she signed as she attempted to look around me

"Jesus, G. You can't even pretend like you're happy to see your brother?"

She rolled her eyes and shook her head as a smile blossomed across her lips. *"I've known you my whole life.*

I'm excited to meet the woman who has finally stolen my brother's heart."

I smiled back at my sister as I felt the depth of her words. She had heard enough about Harper and as soon as she had a free weekend, she was practically begging me to come visit. We usually tried to get together whenever we could, but both of our schedules had been so busy lately, neither of us were at fault.

Harper was nervous as hell to meet my sister. It was a big thing for both of us and she talked about it all night. She was relatively quiet this morning and I didn't press the issue. Instead, I tried to just make the day easier for her to try and help with her anxiety.

"She is getting changed, but wait out here while I go check on her," I signed back to G.

She nodded. *"I'll go make myself at home with Ballsy in the guest room."*

Giana pushed past me and just as she was stepping into the hallway, Harper came out of my room. Her hair was pulled up in a ponytail, her face free of makeup. She was wearing a coral-colored sweater and a pair of black leggings. Her eyes widened for a moment as she was standing face to face with my sister and I watched her expression grow soft. Her eyes were warm as she smiled.

Giana lifted her hand to wave and I watched Harper do the same as she softly said hi and introduced herself. She knew G wasn't able to hear the words she spoke, but she could read her lips.

Harper looked over to me and back at Giana who

was now turning around to look at me. *"Tell her to come with me while I unpack my things."*

I swallowed hard and shook my head. I was suddenly self-conscious of the massive ball of tape I had stored away in my guest room that Harper didn't know about. *"She doesn't know about Ballsy."*

Giana's eyes widened. *"Are you seriously going to be weird about it now?"* She huffed and waved for Harper while pulling out a notepad from her purse. She wrote something on it and showed it to Harper. Harper glanced back at me with a smile before she followed my sister down the hall.

I lingered for a moment, not sure if I should follow after them or not. Harper told me she didn't really know ASL which wasn't unusual for most people. Unless you had someone who had hearing difficulties in your life or had a passion for the language, many people didn't know how to communicate using it.

Giana had adjusted through life by carrying around a small notebook or using her phone to get messages across to people who couldn't communicate with her via sign language. A part of me wanted to go in and see what they were talking about. G wasn't overbearing, but I had a feeling she would be asking Harper as many questions as she could get out.

And then there was Ballsy. I wasn't necessarily ashamed of him by any means. I just wasn't sure if Harper would understand his significance or if she would think I was completely fucking weird and something was seriously wrong with me.

Which I supposed could be debatable.

I moved into the living room and sat down on the couch, kicking my feet up as I turned on the TV and flipped to ESPN. There was a talk show on and I just let it take my attention instead of worrying about my sister and my girl in the other room. I stared at the screen and it wasn't long before they were coming down the hall.

G had a smirk on her face and she walked past the living room and into the kitchen instead of talking to me. Harper came in and sat down on the couch beside me. I slung my arm around the tops of her shoulders.

"So, I'm supposed to ask you about that ball of tape you keep in your guest room."

I knew this was coming.

"Yeah, that's Ballsy," I said with a shrug of indifference.

Harper angled her head to the side with a smile. "It has a name?"

A chuckle rumbled in my chest as the nervousness I previously felt quickly dissipated. "Yep. When I was a kid, I used to leave balls of tape all over the place. My mom would get so annoyed as she collected them and when she gave them to me, I started to build a bigger ball by combining them all."

I watched Harper's expression transform. There was nothing but warmth and softness in her gaze as she waited for me to continue.

"It became a tradition. Every season, I would start a new ball of tape and collect it the entire season." I paused as the memory of my mother drifted into my mind. "My mom was the one who came up with the name Ballsy. I have no idea where, but it stuck. And then we've had multiple generations of Ballsy since then."

Harper smiled. "I love it. I mean, sure, it's not like everyone has a massive ball of tape sitting in their guest room... but I like it. It's a part of you and who you are."

I stared at her for a moment in disbelief. "You're really not weirded out by it? I mean, it is like a good luck kind of thing in a way."

"I don't judge you for Ballsy," she said with a soft laughter and it was like music to my ears. "It's actually rather impressive and I love the symbolism behind it."

I pulled her close to me as I pressed my lips to her forehead. "Have I told you that I love you?"

"You've been doing that a lot lately."

I smiled as I rested my cheek against the top of her head. "Well, you had better get used to it because I don't plan on ever stopping."

G stepped out into the room and cleared her throat, gaining both of our attention. I turned around to look at her, watching the smile forming on her lip as she saw the two of us sitting there together.

"Did you tell her about Ballsy?" she signed to me as she walked up around the couch to sit with us.

I rolled my eyes at her. "Yes, I told her about Ballsy," I said out loud while signing to my sister. Harper looked over at the two of us. I didn't want her to feel left out while Giana and I were signing back and forth with one another.

Giana moved to sit on the adjacent side of the sectional couch. She turned her direction toward Harper and began to sign as I spoke the words out loud to her. *"So, Harper, tell me all about your photography. Nico has told me a little, but not enough."*

Harper smiled as she looked between the two of us. Her eyes landed on Giana's and she spoke out loud explaining to her about being a sports photographer and her plans for the future. I didn't need to sign for Giana as she read Harper's lips, and watching the interaction between the two of them felt like my heart was melting into a fucking puddle.

What the hell was she doing to me?

I watched G struggle in life with the way people treated her when they found out she was deaf. It was like there was a disconnect with some people and they viewed her as if she were flawed. They didn't know how to properly communicate with her. Instead of speaking to her normally, the way Harper was, they would speak loudly and slowly as if she were stupid and couldn't follow them.

It was sad to watch but I knew it just annoyed Giana more than anything. She wasn't one to let those kinds of people and their ignorance deter her in life. Giana signed to me to relay the message to Harper since Harper wasn't as skilled at reading lips like my sister was.

"That's so interesting," I told Harper for Giana. "I never really knew how intense taking pictures of a sport could be. It sounds like you're really building something with the different clientele outside of sports."

Harper was watching Giana mouth the words as she signed them to me and it was almost as if I weren't even there. I was simply just the voice translating. Harper didn't once look at me like it was the two of us talking. Her focus was solely on Giana.

She smiled again. "I'm really hoping I can get something going so I can quit sports, honestly."

I glanced over at her. "You want to quit completely?"

Harper looked over to me now with a shy smile as she nodded. "I told you it wasn't where my heart was and I've decided it would be best if I left it behind completely." She paused for a moment as something glimmered in her eyes. "The sooner the better, wouldn't you agree?"

My tongue darted out as I wet my lips. "Definitely sooner. As soon as possible, actually."

Harper laughed softly. "Well, I can't do that yet. I need to get more established and finish out the rest of the season."

She had told me already that she didn't want her entire career to be in sports photography, but I didn't realize she meant she wanted to leave it completely. The thought and the possibility had a rush of adrenaline racing through my veins. If she didn't work for the team any longer, then we were free to fully explore this deepening connection between us.

"So, we just have to get through the rest of the season and then I can make you mine?"

Harper's blue eyes shimmered. "Officially, you mean."

"That's right," I murmured as I pulled her close and ignored the sound of my sister clearing her throat. "You're already mine."

Chapter Twenty-five

Harper

As I drove home, I couldn't help but play over how it went meeting Giana for the first time. It felt like it had gone well and she was very likable. I didn't know why I was so nervous about meeting her. She was probably one of the nicest people I had ever met. Although, I wouldn't want to be the one to cross her. I couldn't imagine how she would be if she felt her brother had been done wrong.

The closeness between them brought a smile to my lips. Coming from a family where I was an only child, siblings were always something I had been jealous of. I never had someone in my corner like that and there was a part of me that always felt like I was missing out on something. It was just me growing up and I had spent a lot of time alone unless I was with friends.

Seeing that Nico and Giana had each other, especially after losing his mother, made me feel a sense of peace for them both. He hadn't really told me much about his father, so it sounded like they only had each other left. My heart ached for the two of them but at least they had one another.

Nico insisted that the three of us were going to go to dinner tonight, but I needed to come home to get changed and everything first. We had both been going back and forth between each other's places and it was getting a little annoying. It seemed like I never had the things I needed when I needed them.

My phone vibrated in my hand as I let myself into my apartment. A smile touched my lips when I saw his name and opened his message.

NICO

I made reservations for tonight and we'll be by to pick you up around six.

Let me know that you get home safely, love.

He was something I wasn't used to. I wasn't used to having someone checking up on me to make sure I was okay. I wasn't necessarily estranged from my family, but we weren't close. Nico was always checking to make sure I got home safely and I couldn't help but really feel the sincerity behind his actions.

They spoke so much more than words, yet they were just a different way of him telling me he really did love me.

HARPER

I just got inside my apartment.

There was no hesitation before he texted me back immediately.

NICO

Good. I miss you.

I tried to stifle the laughter that bubbled in my throat. I shook my head while I collected some clothing and headed into the bathroom to get into the shower.

HARPER

You just saw me and you'll see me again in a few hours.

NICO

That only makes me miss you more.
Can I just come over now?

His words did something to my heart and I wasn't sure it was a feeling I should trust. He had proved himself to be trustworthy. He was nothing like my ex and I knew that now. I just was afraid of the way he made me feel. Things like that were always too good to be true.

Maybe that wasn't true. Maybe I just needed to let go of my fear since I had already decided to take the risk with him.

HARPER

What about your sister?

I set my phone down as I turned on the shower and undressed before his next message came through.

NICO

She knows how to get an Uber. She can meet us at the restaurant.

I half smiled, half frowned as I shook my head at my phone.

HARPER

> Be a good brother and hang out with your sister. You'll see me soon enough.

NICO

> Fine. But I'm dropping her off at my place after dinner and I want you to myself tonight.

I smiled.

HARPER

> Sounds like the perfect plan.

Setting my phone back down on the counter, I stepped into the steam and felt the hot water hitting my back as I turned around underneath it. Closing my eyes, I moved my head back and let it run down my long locks.

My thoughts drifted to him as I washed my body and my hair. He had become my addiction. I was either with him or if I wasn't with him, he was what I was thinking about. He occupied every inch and every corner of my mind. Nico was here to stay.

Nico was the most unexpected thing I'd ever had happen to me and I wouldn't have traded any of it for anything else. Even if things weren't going to turn out as I had hoped they would...

———

As I sat in the front seat of Nico's car, he slid his hand into mine and I looked over at him as he pulled out of the parking lot. It was just the two of us and I was surprised when I got into the car and didn't see his sister. He claimed that she said she didn't want to go out tonight, but a part of me was questioning whether or not she really meant that.

"You didn't talk Giana out of coming to dinner with us, did you?"

Nico chuckled softly as we sped down the street. "I promise you I didn't. The thought definitely crossed my mind but she was the one who beat me to it."

"She really just didn't feel like going out, or what was her actual reason?" I quizzed him.

He shrugged. "She said she was tired and didn't feel like going out tonight. I honestly think she just wanted to give the two of us some time alone, but I wasn't going to argue with her on it. G is a big girl and can make her own decisions. If she didn't feel like coming along, that's on her."

I studied the side of his face. "The two of you don't really see each other that much, though, right?"

He shook his head as he glanced over at me. "Maybe every month or so. It just depends on what we both have going on in our schedules." He paused for a moment. "Did you not want to get dinner with me tonight?"

"Nope. Why would I want to get dinner with you?" I rolled my eyes at him as I laughed quietly and shook my head. "Of course I want to. I just didn't want your sister to feel like she was left out or not welcome or anything."

"I think she would have felt more left out if she came with us," he said with a wink as he turned his attention back to the road. "I'm sure she didn't want to feel like a third wheel or anything like that."

I contemplated his words. "I don't want her to feel like that. We're not that bad, are we?"

"It's not like we're ever around anyone else, so I can't really say."

"You have a valid point," I agreed with a smile. We settled into a comfortable silence as we continued to the restaurant that Nico still hadn't told me about yet. When we pulled into the quaint town that was about half an hour outside of the city, it gave me a weird sense of nostalgia.

Nico parked his car along the street and came over to my side to help me out. My hand was back in his and we were walking down the sidewalk as the brisk air made my cheeks tingle.

"This reminds me of the town my grandmother lived in," I told him with a smile as I turned to look up at him. "It was a small town like this, where everything was within walking distance. Super safe, super quaint. Almost like out of a storybook. Everyone knew each other and it just felt like home."

His eyes were on mine as he looked at me while we continued to walk. "I thought you said you lived in Denver?"

"I did," I told him as he came to a stop outside of one of the smaller buildings. "My grandmother lived in a small town outside of the city. I used to spend a lot of time visiting with her and it was honestly my favorite. It didn't feel nearly as congested and it was almost as if time didn't exist."

"What happened that you don't go there anymore?"

I shrugged as sadness settled into my bones. "After she had passed away, my father ended up selling her house. My parents didn't see a purpose in keeping it. I haven't been able to bring myself to go back and visit there since."

Nico was silent for a moment. "Would you ever consider going back or is that somewhere you'd never like to visit again?"

That was a thought that had lingered in my mind since she passed away five years ago. It was a thought I had kept to myself and never once muttered a single word to anyone about. It was more like a dream—and probably an unattainable one at this point.

"I always told myself that one day I would buy her old house and move there."

He tilted his head to the side. "Yet, you moved here instead?"

My chest rose as I sucked in a deep breath. "The property wasn't for sale and I didn't have the money to buy a house right out of college." I exhaled and cast my eyes to the ground, suddenly feeling embarrassed. "It was more of a dream, not something I really believed would ever happen."

Nico's hand slid under my chin and he lifted my chin to look up at him. "Don't ever doubt yourself, love. You can make anything happen. Your dreams can come true." He pressed his soft lips to mine in a quick kiss. "Come on, let's get inside before they end up canceling our reservation because we didn't show up."

He pulled me along with him and I followed him inside. The lights were dim and light classical music played in the background. The aroma of garlic drifted through the air and I closed my eyes as I inhaled deeply.

"Italian?" I asked him as we walked up to the host who was waiting for us.

Nico nodded. "They have the best food here."

He gave his name and we were led over to a table for two. We were seated along an ivy-covered wall with a small candle burning between the two of us. It was incomparable to the actual fire that was burning between us. Nico folded his hands on the table and his left dimple was showing as he smiled at me.

"Both of my parents are Italian, so we grew up eating the authentic shit." He drifted for a moment, like he was caught in a memory. "My mother actually came here from Italy as a kid. She used to make her own pasta and I haven't tasted anything quite as good since. But this place—they have the closest to hers that I could find."

I watched him carefully for a moment as his gaze drifted and grew distant before he returned to me. "Do you talk to your father much? You don't say much about him."

His face fell but he quickly recovered as he attempted to keep his face neutral. What he couldn't shield was the pain that washed through his blue irises.

"We talk occasionally," he said with a simplicity that didn't match his eyes.

Silence settled between us and my heart pounded in my chest. I didn't want to push the topic if he didn't want to talk about it. Our server appeared and took our order for drinks and appetizers before disappearing from the table.

"He loved her more than anyone in the world, including G and I." Nico's voice was hoarse and he caught me off guard. "When she died, we lost him too. He was still here and present, but he really wasn't. He was vacant and distant. The day my mother passed away, we lost both of our parents."

My heart broke for him as I watched the moisture grow in his eyes. There was such a sadness to him, such a vulnerability as he spoke of his father. It was evident he probably hadn't expressed this to anyone else and it was taking such a toll on him to even entertain the thoughts.

"He follows my hockey career, but he's never been to any of my games," he said quietly with his voice thick with emotion. "I don't think he ever will be without her. Giana and I kind of just knew we had to accept the fact that he was living with a broken soul that would never be repaired. I think the only reason he's still here is because of us, even though he would much rather be with her wherever that is."

I reached across the table and took his hands in my own. "I'm so sorry, Nico. For everything that you've gone through."

"It's okay," he said as he pushed a sad smile onto his

face. "It's something I've accepted and I'm beginning to understand why he would feel the way he does." He stared at me, his eyes piercing my soul. "I know the love he had for her because I can feel it too. For you, Harper. All for fucking you."

His words ran through my veins and tangled themselves around my heart. The pads of his thumbs were soft as they stroked the backs of my hands and his eyes were trained on mine.

"Don't ever leave me, Harper," he said, his voice barely audible. "I don't know that I would survive your destruction."

I stared back at him as I was lost in his stormy eyes. He had already pulled me in deep and there was no way I was ever swimming to the surface again. He thought he wouldn't survive my destruction, but he had no idea what losing him would do to me.

"Never," I promised him.

And that scared me more than anything.

Chapter Twenty-six

Nico

Harper settled in the passenger seat of my car as we drove down the street of the quaint little town. We stayed at the restaurant talking about our lives until they were getting ready to close. It was late into the night already and Harper yawned as she curled her legs up onto the seat. She turned to look at me with a tired smile touching her lips.

"Thank you for dinner tonight," she said softly as her eyes glimmered through the darkness of the night. Every streetlamp we passed cast its light across her face. She was absolutely breathtaking and I could spend the rest of my time in this life staring at her.

I smiled back at my girl. "Of course, love."

Her eyes were still on mine and I was alternating between looking at the road and looking at her. "Don't tell your sister, but I'm glad she didn't come. I like my time with you."

"You can have all of my time, Harper. Every second,

every minute, every fucking hour. They all belong to you."

She sat up a little straighter, the smile still on her lips as she glanced out through the windshield. I watched her face abruptly fall and her eyes widened before she pointed at me. "Oh my god, Nico! Look out!"

I tore my eyes away from her and watched in horror as someone was pulling out from a side road in front of me. My body reacted and it was as if time had slowed down. As I slammed my foot down on the brakes, I jerked the wheel to the left, attempting to veer away from the car. My tires squealed loudly as the brakes locked up and we slid across the road.

We just narrowly missed the car that pulled out, but it didn't stop us from crashing into the guardrail on the other side of the road. The sound of metal crunching was loud and piercing. Harper yelled out as we bounced off the guardrail. My head jerked with such force. The airbags were blasting out at us and the car finally stopped. Silence settled in the air around us and my mind was jarred from the impact.

My head felt like it was swimming through the thickest sludge and I slowly looked around. All of the airbags were deployed and my body ached from the impact of the accident. Other than that, I couldn't tell if anything was really wrong with me. I didn't care anyway. All I wanted was to make sure she was okay.

And my stomach sank when I saw her sitting in her seat with her head hanging.

"Harper," I said her name as I reached over for her. My seat belt tightened around my body, constricting me momentarily before I could get to her. I slowly lifted her head. There was a bright red abrasion on the top right side of her forehead, probably from hitting the window or something. "Harper, wake up."

I slid my finger under her nose and could feel her soft breaths. Relief rushed through my body as I realized she was at least alive. But she was still unconscious and I needed to get help. Suddenly the door behind me groaned loudly as it was pulled open. I didn't bother to look over my shoulder as I was trying to get mine and Harper's seat belts unbuckled.

"Are you okay?" a rough voice said from behind me. "I already called 911 and they should be here any minute."

The seat belt finally clicked and I ripped it away from Harper's body. I finally looked over my shoulder at the older man and cut my eyes at him. "Why the fuck would you pull out in front of someone like that? That could have killed her."

He shook his head and his eyes were filled with regret. I instantly felt guilty. The wrinkles were visible on his face and they cut deep as his gray eyebrows pulled together. "I'm so sorry. My eyes aren't what they once were and I didn't see your car. Please let me help you."

"Maybe that's a sign that you shouldn't be fucking driving then."

He winced at my harsh words but I wasn't about to take them back. Not now, not when Harper was unconscious because of him pulling out in front of us. It was a mistake he never should have made.

"Please let me help you out of the car," he insisted. "We shouldn't move her, just in case she injured her neck or something."

My eyes were wild as I stared at him. "I'm not leaving her in the car."

"Nico?" Her voice was so quiet and if my senses weren't heightened in this moment, I would have missed it completely.

I whipped my head back around to her. "Oh, love," I breathed as a smile pulled on my lips and relief flooded me. "Are you okay? Does anything hurt?"

Her eyes were glazed over as she opened them to look at me. I watched her try to nod and she winced as she lifted her hand up to her head. "My head. I think I hit it on something."

"Shh," I murmured as I moved her hand away from the bleeding cut on her forehead. Sirens sounded in the distance and the sound grew louder as they moved closer to us. "It will all be okay, love."

Her lips parted like she was going to say something but she quickly closed them and closed her eyes. It was like the time that was suspended was suddenly cata-pulted into fast forward. We were surrounded by two fire trucks, an ambulance, and a few police cars. Everyone was moving quickly and it was a bustle of commotion.

I was able to get myself out of the car as I felt stiff-ness in my legs. I watched as the paramedics assessed Harper and helped her out. She was a little unsteady on her feet but her eyes were a little clearer than they were when she first opened them. They helped her walk over to the ambulance and I had to answer questions from the police officer while the older man spoke to one of the other officers.

After we finished up and the tow truck pulled up to take away my totaled car, I rushed over to the ambulance where they had Harper sitting on the stretcher inside. Her gaze lifted to mine as I stepped up inside.

"Is everything okay?"

Harper nodded slowly and closed her eyes as she winced from the pain. "They want me to go to the hospital just to be sure."

One of the paramedics stepped beside Harper and urged her to lay down. "You need to rest right now." The woman turned around to face me and motioned for me to step outside of the ambulance. "We suspect she has a concussion. We're going to take her to the hospital so they can check and make sure that is all it is."

I swallowed roughly over the lump lodged in my throat. "I need to go with her."

The woman nodded in understanding. "We will let you ride along with us to take her in and we also need you to get checked out too."

"I'm fine," I assured her as I felt the twinge of pain running down my leg. "I don't need anyone to worry about me. I just want to make sure she's okay."

She shook her head at me. "The choice is ultimately yours, but they're going to insist you get checked. Also, considering the fact that you're not putting weight on your right leg is a sign that something is wrong. We're leaving in two minutes, so please be ready to go."

She moved back to the ambulance without giving

me a chance to say anything else to her. There was nothing I really needed to say. She was right—I needed to get my leg looked at. There was no way I could safely skate with the pain I was feeling. As I turned around I found the old man lingering. I sucked in a deep breath and shoved my hands in my front pockets as I approached him.

"Is she okay?" he asked as I stepped up to him. There was a hint of worry in his tired features and his voice was strained. The guilt was evident, yet I knew we were both at fault.

"They're going to take her in to make sure there's nothing wrong, but she'll be okay." I paused for a moment as I let out the breath I didn't realize I was holding. "I apologize for what I said earlier. I shouldn't have been so crass and rude to you. You were only trying to help and you didn't intentionally pull out in front of us for this to happen."

His chin wobbled a bit and his eyes grew damp as he sucked his lips in between his teeth. I watched his throat bob as he swallowed and nodded. "You don't have to apologize to me, son. There was no harm done on your end and I would have reacted the same way if something like that would have happened to my Eleanor."

My eyes dropped down to his hands and I watched as he toyed with the wedding band on his thick finger. My gaze met his and I gave him a small smile. No other words needed to be spoken between us because he knew. A complete stranger knew the exact feelings that were racing through my body at the moment of the accident.

I looked back to the ambulance as the man hobbled away. They had the engine running and they were getting ready to take her to the hospital. My footsteps were quick as I rushed across the road to her and I hopped on just before the woman pulled the doors shut.

I moved to Harper's side and sat down on the bench as I slid both of my hands around hers. Harper turned her head to look at me, her bright blue eyes colliding with mine.

"Nico," she whispered. "What are you doing? You can't come to the hospital with me."

"The fuck I can't," I growled as I cut my eyes at her. "You're hurt. I'm not letting you out of my fucking sight."

Her throat bobbed and a worried look passed through her irises. "Nico," she started as she tried to argue, but I shook my head at her.

"This isn't up for discussion, love. I don't give a shit about what happens or who sees us. I'm not leaving your side."

She let out a deep breath and her expression was grim. "Goddammit."

"I know, love," I murmured as she closed her eyes and tightened her hand around mine. This was either going to be the end of us or the end of her career. Either way, someone was going to catch wind of this and there was only so much denying the both of us could do. "I know…"

Chapter Twenty-seven

Harper

The stretcher was smooth on the linoleum floor of the hospital. The entire emergency room was loud with the noise of other patients and the staff consistently on their toes. I watched in a daze as people rushed past us. My head felt like it was swimming while simultaneously pounding. The blood on my forehead had since dried and turned into a scab that felt like a piece of glue stuck to my skin. It felt taut and was really sore.

They wheeled me into a room and Nico was right there walking beside me the entire time. A nurse stopped him at the door as she put her hand up in front of him.

"I'm sorry, sir, but we need to check to make sure it's okay if you're back here with her."

His eyes went wild and his jaw clenched. "I'm not going anywhere without her." There was a coldness in his tone and it was almost too calm. It was as if he were a volcano that was getting ready to erupt. Like the calm before the storm.

The nurse glanced over at me and looked back at him. "Please wait outside for one moment. If you don't cooperate, I will have to call security."

Nico's gaze flashed to mine and I nodded at him. He let out an exasperated sigh and stepped out of her way. The nurse pulled the door shut behind her and stepped inside the room. "It's protocol for us to ask questions in private in regards to your safety."

My eyebrows pulled together. "Okay..."

She went through a series of questions, all of which I answered honestly. After she deemed it was safe to let him back into the room, he rushed in like a whirlwind and took his spot back by my side. He was standing guard, like he would attack anyone he thought wasn't doing what they should be or if they were a threat to me.

Various nurses and doctors came in to check on me before they decided I needed to get a CAT scan for them to make sure there was no trauma to my brain. Nico's phone began to ring as we were waiting for someone to come take me back. I watched his face fall as he looked at the screen and glanced back at me.

"It's Wes," he said with his voice low. "Fuck."

"Answer it."

Nico frowned, but he accepted the call and held his phone up to his ear. His body instantly grew rigid as he listened to Wes rambling through the speaker. "No, we're fine. We're at the hospital right now for Harper to get checked."

His jaw was clenched as he listened again and he ran a frustrated hand through his hair as he hung his head. His shoulders sagged and something wasn't right. "Who all knows?" He fell silent again. "What the fuck did it say?" Silence again, but his footsteps filled the void as he began to pace. "No. Fuck. That's not what happened at all."

My head was still pounding and there was a feeling of dread building in my stomach from the way Nico was behaving. I watched the slight limp in his gait and that made me feel even worse. My mind began to race as I played over every possible worst-case scenario in my head.

"Yeah, I'll let you know when we get out of here. Thanks, bro," Nico said quietly to Wes before walking back over to the bed. His eyes instantly found mine. "Someone posted about the accident on Twitter. No one has any idea how anyone found out… but I'm pretty sure everyone knows."

I stared back at him for a moment as the words registered and settled in my mind. "Shit," I mumbled as I realized what this really meant. My job was officially in jeopardy. Nico's eyes were laced with concern and I reached out for him, for his hand. His palm was warm against mine. "We'll worry about it all later. You need to get your leg looked at."

Nico was silent for a moment. "Fuck my leg. What happens to us?"

"What do you mean?" I demanded, just as the radiology technician stepped into the room. "This changes nothing between us, Nico. I'll figure it out."

His eyes softened. "No, you won't. We will —*together*."

I held his gaze, feeling his words as they settled deep within my soul. There was nothing but love radiating from the way he was looking at me and I could literally feel his words. We were no longer separate entities. We were in this together and we would figure it all out together instead of alone.

As the technician wheeled me away, I felt Nico's absence as soon as his hand left mine. He was always in a better position when it came to our little secret we had between us. If anyone found out, Nico would always be safe because they weren't going to jeopardize his career because of a little scandal. I was much more expendable than he was.

There were plenty of other photographers out there and they didn't need me. I'd be easily replaced and I already knew that was the position I would find myself in. I knew this would eventually blow up in our faces, I just didn't know when.

———

Nico went and got his knee checked out as they finished up my tests. They determined that we were both fine. I had a concussion and he had some swelling in his knee that he would need to rest before he could skate again. Nico called Wes and he showed up at the hospital to pick us up and take us home.

"How are you feeling, Harper?" Wes asked me as I climbed into the back seat of his car. Nico followed behind me and I gave him a questioning look. "What am I, your chauffeur?"

Nico's eyes sliced to Wes's through the rearview mirror. "Just drive please."

"I'm all right," I answered Wes's question as he looked to me before he started to drive. "My head is just killing me so the sooner you can get us to Nico's the better."

"What about you, man?" Wes probed Nico. "Are you good?"

"I can't play for, like, two weeks and will have to be cleared by the team doctor to be able to get back onto the ice."

"Fuck," Wes mumbled as he shook his head. "I mean, it could be worse. I'm just glad I'm not you and don't have to have that conversation with Coach."

Nico cocked his head. "I'm sure he already knows since it seems like word spread relatively quickly."

Wes shrugged. "Better you tell him about it yourself. He's already going to be pissed, so I don't think it's worth giving him another reason to be unhappy."

"Good point."

I tuned the two of them out as I rested my head on Nico's shoulder. The hospital wasn't far from his apartment and it wasn't long before we were riding up the elevator to his floor. Nico's arm was around my waist, like he thought I was the one who was having trouble walking. As we stepped off the elevator, I swayed slightly and was grateful for his overprotective arm.

He kept me steady and his sister was pacing the hall as we stepped deeper into his apartment. She began to move her hands around, signing in a frenzy. I couldn't understand what she was saying, but Nico's eyes were tracking each movement she made.

"I'm sorry I didn't let you know as soon as it happened," he spoke out loud so she could read his lips with his arm still around me. "We're both fine. My knee is a little banged up and Harper has a concussion."

I gave Giana a small smile as she looked at me for a moment. She signed something else to Nico that I didn't understand.

"Do you need anything?" Nico asked me for her.

I shook my head. "No, thank you. I think I just need to go lay down and rest my head."

Giana signed while Nico translated. "She said for us to go get comfortable and let her take care of everything."

She stepped out of the way while Nico limped the two of us back to his bedroom. He walked me over to his bed and helped me on as I climbed up. I looked down at my clothing and realized I didn't have anything here since I had taken all of my things home earlier in the day to wash.

Nico was already walking over to his closet and came back with one of his t shirts. "Here, love," he murmured as he handed it to me. I set it down on the bed and stripped down to my underwear before pulling the shirt over my head.

He had already stripped down to his boxers and grabbed a pair of basketball shorts that he put on. I settled under the covers in his plush bed and he crawled in with me. He pulled me into his arms until I was flush against him with my head on his chest.

"Today scared the shit out of me," he whispered into my hair as he held me close. "When I saw you were unconscious, I swear my entire fucking world stopped. The Earth stopped spinning and my heart stopped beating."

"I'm not going anywhere," I promised him, meaning every single word. "We're both okay and we have each other."

Nico fell silent for a breath. "I can't lose you, Harper."

"You're not going to."

"But we don't know what is going to happen with your job or any of that shit," he reminded me, his tone tense and his words heavy. I could feel the turmoil radiating from him and I tightened my arm around his waist.

"I don't want to think about it right now."

"Okay, love," he said softly as he stroked my hair. "Go to sleep and rest your head. I'll be right here when you wake up."

I smiled against his chest as exhaustion settled inside me. My eyelids were growing heavier by every passing second and I knew I needed to sleep. It was what my body needed to heal and I couldn't fight it any longer. Nico's warmth enveloped me and it wasn't long before I was drifting off into a dream world where our problems no longer existed.

Chapter Twenty-eight

Nico

Rolling over in bed, my eyes were still closed as I slid my hand across the mattress. I was expecting to feel Harper's warm body against mine but when I didn't, I felt around for her in the bed with my hands. The side she was lying on was still warm, but she wasn't there. I lifted my eyelids and lifted my head to look for her.

Where the hell did she go?

Panic slid through my veins and I couldn't help the feeling of dread that built in my stomach. After the accident, this newfound anxiety had decided to enter my mind. I was terrified of losing Harper. It wasn't that I didn't realize her importance in my life before yesterday—it was just one of those moments that really put things into perspective. And Harper was the one I knew I couldn't live without.

I climbed out of bed and as I was walking to the door of my bedroom, a wave of relief fell over me as I heard her voice just outside. Thank God. Reaching for the doorknob, I turned it and pulled the door open. Harper was sitting on the hallway floor with her back against the wall across from my door. Her gaze lifted to meet mine as she saw me and I raised an eyebrow at her.

"Yes, of course," she said quietly into the phone. I moved into the hall and sat down across from her as I saw the worry lingering in her eyes. "I agree that we should have a meeting to discuss this matter in person rather than over the phone."

I glanced down the hall as my guest bedroom door opened up and my sister stepped out. She looked at both of us like we were insane and quickly signed to me. *What the hell are you guys doing on the floor?*

I shrugged. *I found Harper out here so I decided I'd sit with her.*

Giana stared at the two of us for a moment. *You guys are kind of weird. Can I talk to you for a minute?*

I looked back to Harper who was listening intently to whatever the other person was saying to her through the phone. Judging by what I had heard of her conversation, I was assuming it had to do with the small scandal we had caused. I swallowed roughly and climbed to my feet as I followed my sister out into the kitchen.

Giana took a seat at the island. *So, you can say no... but I was wondering if I could stay here a little while longer.*

"*Absolutely,*" I signed back to her. "*You know my home is yours and you can stay as long as you want.*"

She pursed her lips and fiddled with her fingers for a moment. *I don't want to go back home. I meant to tell you sooner, but I want to live here, closer to you. There's nothing for me in Tampa and I really just needed to come home."*

I assessed my sister for a moment. *"Did something happen? Is everything okay?"*

She nodded and smiled. *"Everything is fine. I just think it's time for me to start living my own life the way I want to."*

"You can stay here for as long as you need or want to, G," I told her with nothing but honesty. My doors would always be open for my little sister. *"What about Dad?"*

"What about him?" she signed back and shook her head. *"We literally live, like, fifteen minutes from one another and I rarely see him. I doubt he'll even notice that I'm gone."*

Her words struck my heart and I felt bad. I left as soon as I was drafted, but Giana had no reason to leave. She went to college in Tampa and lived with our father during that period of time. Since she had graduated and started working as a marine biologist, she was able to get her own apartment, but she didn't venture far away. I knew part of her stayed because she was worried about him.

Orchid Beach was always our home. When I went off to college, our parents moved to Tampa because my mother wanted to be on the gulf side. Ironically, she never made it back to our hometown before she passed away. And this was the only place I wanted to be because of her memory.

It just seemed like maybe Giana had finally realized we were never going to be much in our father's eyes because we weren't our mother. Some people just can't move on in their lives after losing the most important piece of themselves. Loving Harper made me empathize with him more and I understood. But as his son, that didn't make anything any better. It didn't make me feel better or any less pain for my sister.

I would like to think that if Harper and I had children involved and something happened to her, I would hold on to them as tightly as I possibly could. They would be the only lasting thing from her. Almost like her legacy or her living memory. I guessed that our father just couldn't see past his heartbreak to realize he still had us.

"I'll only stay until I get a job and can find my own place," Giana told me as she broke through my thoughts and her hands moving caught my attention again.

I nodded at her. *"As long as you need, G. You're the only real family I have and I'll always be here for whatever you need."*

She smiled at me and I watched as a wave of curiosity passed through her expression. *"Did you hear that Malakai was back too?"*

I slowly cocked my head to the side. *"Since when? He didn't say anything to me about it."*

"You still talk to him?" my sister signed back to me with a surprised look on her face.

Malakai Barclay was my best friend growing up. He came from an extremely wealthy family, but he was also troubled. He wasn't one who openly spoke about his problems, except to one person. Winter Reign. Malakai never really told me what was going on between the two of them at the time, but when she left to go to college in Vermont, Malakai left too.

From what I knew, he didn't follow her. He was off chasing his dreams of being a professional golfer and getting as far away from his abusive father as possible.

"We talk occasionally, but you know how he is," I told her with a shrug.

Malakai was like a closed book. We had kept in touch over the years, but it was relatively scarce. He knew I was back in Orchid Beach so it surprised me that he didn't let me know he had returned as well.

"Maybe text him and see if he wants to get together."

I stared at my sister for a moment. Knowing Malakai, he would probably blow me off. With him, there was always a darkness that crept just beneath the surface. I was happy for him that he was doing well in life, but Malakai had the type of demons you couldn't outrun. I could only hope for his sake that he had learned how to fight them instead.

"I'll have to do that."

As I pulled out my phone, I unlocked the screen and went to my messages to send Malakai a text. It was short and to the point and I was surprised when he responded almost immediately.

NICO

Hey man, I heard you were back in town. Let's catch up sometime.

MALAKAI

Drinks tonight at The Lounge? Meet me there around eight.

NICO

Sounds good. I'll see you then.

"He wants to meet up tonight at The Lounge," I signed to my sister.

Giana smiled at me just as Harper wandered into the kitchen with us. She paused in the doorway and I turned back to look at her. "I'm sorry, I didn't mean to interrupt," she said apologetically with a small smile.

I held out my hand, extending my arm for her as I smiled back at her and shook my head. Harper stepped close to me and I hooked my arm around the tops of her shoulders as she slid against my side. "Absolutely not, love. Giana was just telling me her plans about wanting to move here. She's going to stay with me until she can find a job and get her own place."

Harper's smile was bright and she looked over to my sister. "This is amazing news!" She genuinely looked happy as she continued to smile at Giana.

Giana nodded and smiled back at her while she began to sign in response as I translated for her. *"I can't wait to get to know you better and spend more time with you guys."*

"I can't wait either. I'm actually still relatively new here to the city, so it will be nice to have another friend."

Listening to the two of them had my heart feeling like it was going to burst from my chest. Giana wasn't a mean person, but we were both similar in the way that we were protective about the people who meant the most to us—and I was one of those people to her. When

I was in high school and college dating other girls, G never approved of any of them. She knew none of them were going, so she didn't really give those girls the time of day.

Seeing how she was with Harper made me realize that she knew how serious this was too. She knew Harper was it for me. There had never been anyone else quite like her in my life before. Giana knew she was the real deal.

I turned my attention back to Harper. "Was everything okay with whoever you were talking to on the phone?"

Harper's shoulders sagged a bit and she shook her head. "I don't think so." She paused for a moment as she stepped out from under my arm and grabbed herself a cup of coffee. "It was Phillip, the head of media. He wants to have a meeting on Tuesday before the game to discuss things."

Dread rolled in the pit of my stomach and Harper leaned against the counter as she sipped from her mug. Giana looked between the two of us and I spoke the words she signed out loud for her.

"G wants to know what there is to discuss."

Harper shrugged and faced my sister as she spoke, even though she was talking to the two of us. "He knows about the accident and that the two of us were together. I'm assuming he's probably going to either fire me or make me resign and go away quietly."

"Shit," I mumbled as I hung my head. I only let myself feel the blow from reality before looking back to her. "I'm coming to the meeting with you."

Harper's eyes widened. "No. There's no reason for you to go. This is about my job, and I'm sure you'll have to answer to your coach and everyone already."

Her words reminded me that I needed to call Coach Anderson to talk to him and see who else I needed to deal with. What a fucking mess. It wasn't like either of us were a threat to each other's jobs. Hell, while we were both working, there was no way we could really even bother each other. There was always a sheet of glass separating us. Harper didn't distract me from playing hockey.

"This is all just fucking bullshit," I growled as I planted my hands on the counter. "Let me talk to them and explain things. Maybe if I come along and say something it will save your job."

Harper stared back at me for a moment. "What is it that you think you could possibly do? How are you going to save my job?"

"I don't know," I shrugged, feeling absolutely helpless at that moment. "There has to be something I can do. I told you I would protect you, love. Please let me do that."

Giana tapped on the counter to get both of our attention before signing, *"I don't think there's anything you can do to help her, Nico. I know you think that being a player on the team that it will make a difference, but they're not going to listen to you."*

"She's right," Harper said quietly after I finished translating. "I'm sure we're not the first to get involved like this or the last. But think about it... If they were to let us slide, they would have to extend the same grace to other people too. There's nothing we can do about it except accept our consequences for our actions."

I shook my head, refusing to accept it. "At least just let me come along."

"It will look worse if we show up together."

"Please, Harper," I practically pleaded with her. "I need to at least try to fix things."

There was a deep-seated need inside of me to ensure she was safe, and that included her job. I knew I was being a little irrational and both of them were right. I wasn't necessarily sure I would be able to change the board's rules that strictly prohibited relationships like this, but I had to try. I promised Harper this wouldn't happen and here we were.

Her chest rose as she inhaled deeply and I watched it fall as she released her breath. "You can't always fix everything, Nico," she said with her voice soft and gentle as her eyes searched mine. "But I'll let you try."

"Thank you, love," I told her as I stepped to her to wrap my arms around her waist.

She looked up at me. "I need to go back to my place sometime today."

"I'll come with you," I told her without any hesitation as I just invited myself along. I was still feeling shook-up and didn't want to be away from her if I didn't have to be. My sister would be fine here without me, especially since she was going to be living here now too.

She smiled at me and shook her head. "You don't have to do that."

"I know I don't, but I want to," I told her as I pressed my lips to her forehead.

"Okay," she agreed softly as she wrapped her arms tighter around me.

I knew I was never going to be able to let her go.

And I was never going to let anything tear us apart.

Chapter Twenty-nine

Nico

After we had gotten back to Harper's apartment, I told her about the plans I had made with Malakai. I instantly felt like an asshole, considering the information she shared with me about her call with Phillip. I should have stayed in with her, but she insisted I go meet Malakai. She declined when I invited her along.

Harper was the most important part of my life. I wanted her involved in every aspect, every space of it, but she was adamant about staying home. She said something about how I needed to catch up with my friend without her. There was also a look of exhaustion that had settled into her features and she needed some time to herself to process the news she had just received.

As I stepped into the bar, it was already crowded and most of the tables were occupied. I pushed my way past some of the groups of people that were standing

271

around, drinking and talking. When I reached the bar, I paused for a moment and scanned the backs of the heads sitting in front of me.

Toward the very end, I caught sight of his dirty blond hair as he tipped his head back and sipped his beer. It was a little longer than the last time I had seen him. It was a mess of tousled waves that rested just above his eyebrows.

As he turned his head to the side and spotted me from across the bar, he gave me a swift nod. No wave, no smile. That was Malakai Barclay.

We were a peculiar pair of friends when we were younger. It wasn't often that any light shone through the darkness that cloaked Malakai; he was generally more reserved and quiet. We were a stark contrast to one another, but I suppose that was why our friendship worked.

There was a seat that was empty next to Malakai and I walked over and slid onto it as I turned to face the bartender. My legs were tucked beneath the bar and I folded my arms in front of me as I turned to look at my old friend.

Malakai glanced over at me, his stare blank with a hardness settled in his jaw. He had filled out over the years and you could tell he had been working out to stay fit, considering his blossoming golf career. The coldness was still enveloping him like it always had.

"How have you been, Kai?" I inquired as I waited for the bartender. "It's been years. You look good, dude."

He lifted an eyebrow. "Thanks. I've been all right. How about you?"

I shrugged dismissively. "You know how it goes. Busy with hockey and shit."

"I can only imagine." His voice almost sounded thoughtful for a fraction of a second, but Kai was never one to give much away. He was always slightly distant, but something about him made it feel like he was completely disconnected from it all.

The bartender walked over and I ordered a beer before turning my attention back to Malakai. "I had no idea you were going to be back in town. What brought you back? Golf?"

Kai lifted his beer to his lips and absentmindedly stared at the TV hung above the bar. "Just some unfinished business."

I stared at the side of his face for a moment, taking in his appearance. There was a tiredness that had settled into the corners of his eyes. Even though he was in his mid-twenties, you could tell the demons he had been battling had taken a toll on him.

"Are you staying at your parents' place?"

"Fuck no," he ground out the words as he looked over at me. "I have a condo in town."

His anger wasn't directed at me, and it was valid. After the shit he went through not living up to his father's expectations, I felt like an asshole for even asking that he would stay at their place. His last statement took me by surprise. "I didn't know you had a place here."

Kai shrugged and drained the rest of his beer. "Sorry

I've been shit with keeping in touch. You've been busy with hockey and me with golf."

"It's all good," I told him, although I couldn't help but feel like I was talking to a complete stranger. "That's what happens in life. People grow up and grow apart. I haven't been the best at staying in touch either."

He didn't bother responding to that and the silence settled around us for a moment before Kai chose to speak. That was how Kai operated. If he didn't have anything to say, he wasn't going to fill the void with meaningless shit. "Have you settled down yet or are you still fucking anything that moves?"

A laugh spilled from my lips. "First of all, fuck you. I was a horny-ass teenager and liked getting my dick wet." I paused for a moment, watching his mouth twitch, but it didn't develop into a smile. "Surprisingly, I do have a girlfriend and it's unlike anything I've ever experienced before."

"Good for you," he said with a slight sadness in his tone. He wasn't going to elaborate and I wasn't going to pry. Trying to get anything from him was like trying to get water from a dry well. "You deserve to be happy and with someone who is good for you."

I studied his profile again as he grabbed the fresh beer the bartender brought to him. "What about you? Anyone in your life?"

Malakai's jaw tightened and he flexed his tattooed hand in front of him before wrapping it around the bottle. "Nah."

He didn't offer anything more as he took another swig. When we were in high school he had started his collection of tattoos even though his parents didn't approve. When he came home with one on his neck, I'd never forget the way his father threatened to cut the skin from his body. He was a disgrace in their eyes and he wasn't going to disappoint them in that aspect.

He rose up to the challenge and covered his body in tattoos instead.

"What's the unfinished business you're here for?"

Kai continued to stare at the TV. The silence settled between us and I couldn't tell if he didn't hear me over the noise or if he was choosing to ignore me. The silence continued to stretch and it was a few minutes before he finally spoke.

"Winter came back."

My brow furrowed. "Winter Reign?"

Winter was a quiet girl we both went to high school with. Kai was friends with her, but he was never vocal or really public about their friendship. He kept her to himself.

I always had a feeling there was more to it, especially the mornings I picked him up from the end of her driveway. At the time, it seemed like the same thing I was doing, but I never saw Kai with any other girls.

"She's the unfinished business."

His admission took me by surprise. "What happened between the two of you?"

Malakai's grip tightened around his beer. "A fucking lot."

"That's really all you're going to give me?"

He shrugged. "You always knew everything you needed to, Nico. Nothing more and nothing less."

"Sometimes I wonder how we were even friends when I feel like I really didn't know you." I paused for a moment as the irritation began to build. I didn't know if I expected Kai to be different, but he was even more closed off than he once was. "Did anyone actually really know you?"

He turned his head to look at me, his dark eyes piercing mine. "Winter did."

We fell back into silence and the two of us drained our beers. I was used to the silence with Kai, but now I was left with more questions than I had ever had and I knew he was never going to give me the answers.

"I should probably head out," I told him as I paid my tab and rose from my barstool. "If you want to get together again, you know how to get a hold of me."

Kai turned to look at me and nodded as he followed suit and rose to his feet beside me. "I don't imagine I'll be going anywhere anytime soon."

"Good luck with Winter."

His mouth twitched again. "Do yourself a favor and stay the way you are. Don't fuck up whatever you have with your girl like I did with Winter."

He threw a hundred-dollar bill onto the bar and turned around without another word to me. I watched him for a moment, completely perplexed by it all as I watched him disappear into the crowd. I didn't imagine that I would hear from Kai again anytime soon.

He made it clear he was here for one reason—and one reason only—and there wasn't a part of me that blamed him.

Whatever he had with Winter years ago had stuck

with him this long. Knowing my own feelings for Harper, I understood it completely. And I also knew I would never do anything to jeopardize what we had. I would never make whatever mistakes Kai did.

Harper was mine.

And I would spend the rest of my life loving her.

Chapter Thirty

Harper

As I stood in the doorway of my bedroom, I watched Nico as he stirred in his sleep. His face was relaxed and peaceful as he began to softly snore again. I hated leaving him like this, but it was for the best. He was planning on going to that meeting with me tomorrow morning and I couldn't let him do that. There was nothing he could do about the situation we had gotten ourselves into.

There was nothing either of us could do.

I didn't lie to him about the original meeting, I just didn't tell him that I had texted Phillip later yesterday afternoon to move the meeting to today instead. Nico didn't need to come in and save the day. I knew exactly what I needed to do and that was what I was going to do.

Leaving him in my bed, I snuck out of my apartment and headed over to the stadium. My stomach sank and a part of me felt sad knowing this would probably be the last time I would be parking in the media parking lot. It was bound to happen eventually. Things like this only lasted so long before everything imploded.

Now I had to deal with the aftermath and clean up the mess I had made.

Walking into the stadium, I adjusted my clothes as I walked down the hall. It was a short walk to the elevator that took me to the floor where the media room was. It felt like time was moving slowly and I just wanted to get it over with as quickly as I could.

Phillip was already sitting at the table as I walked inside and I could feel the bile rising in my throat. I absolutely hated conflict, but this was one I wasn't going to be able to avoid. He was the only one in the room and that only made me feel worse.

"Hi, Harper," he said with his voice tense as he motioned for me to sit down across from him. "Please take a seat."

I swallowed hard over the lump in my throat and nodded as I did as he said and sat down. "Are we waiting for anyone else?" I asked him, my voice quiet.

He shook his head. "No, that won't be necessary." He took a sip of his water. "Would you like to go first or shall I?"

"I can," I said without any hesitation. It was like ripping off a Band-Aid. The jump was going to be the scariest part of my journey, but it had to be done. "I want to apologize first. I never meant for something like this to happen."

"Yeah, that's usually how it goes." He fell silent and frowned. "I hate to have to let you go, but you understand this goes against our strict rules. Knowing what we do and the fact that it has gotten out to the public, we can no longer employ you as a photographer for the team."

I nodded. "Yes, I understand that."

He stared at me for a moment as his shoulders sagged. "I don't know you well, Harper, but this was honestly unexpected and a bit of a disappointment. You are an extremely talented photographer, so this is really not what I wanted to have to do today."

"I really am sorry, Phillip," I said to him, feeling the deep regret inside. "I never wanted this to happen, but I accept the consequences for what I have done. There is nothing I can do to take it back."

Phillip nodded. "This is effective immediately, so we won't be needing you at the game tomorrow."

"I understand," I responded as we both rose from our seats. There was nothing else to really say. Phillip was my boss and not my friend, so what happened in my life after this moment didn't concern him. "Thank you for the opportunity of working for the team."

"Of course, Harper," he said with a sad smile. "Please take care of yourself and I wish you the best in life."

I thanked him again and felt lighter as I walked out of the media room. I had served my purpose here and it was time for me to close out this chapter of my life. As I stepped into the hallway and the door closed behind me, I glanced over my shoulder once more as I looked back at the room.

This job would always be special to me, even if it

wasn't my career anymore. If I hadn't gotten the job, I wouldn't have ended up in Orchid Beach. And if I weren't here, chances were that I wouldn't have run into Nico that night. I would have never gotten the opportunity to meet him and have him in my life.

It was a bittersweet moment. A part of me didn't want to give it up because this was quite possibly the scariest thing I had ever done. I came in here knowing I would no longer be employed, but I also came here with a plan. It was as if it were that final last push I needed to branch out on my own.

I didn't need to work here anymore. It was time for me to start doing my own thing.

As I reached my car and glanced up at the stadium once more, I pulled out my phone and tapped on Ava's name. She texted me as soon as she heard about the accident and made sure I was okay. She was the one who instantly knew I was with Nico so when I talked to Phillip yesterday, I made sure I let her know we were having an official meeting.

"Hey, girl. What are you doing?" Ava said as she answered the phone.

"Well," I started as I turned the key to bring the engine of my car to life, "I just got fired."

Ava was silent for a beat. "Okay. We knew this was going to happen. It was inevitable. So, what do you have planned next?"

"I'm finally going to follow my dreams," I told her, my voice soft as I didn't fully trust it. Speaking it out into the universe felt weird and almost as if it wasn't reality. "I'm officially starting my own photography business."

"Harper, this is the best news ever!" Ava exclaimed and the excitement was evident in her voice. "I'm so proud of you for finally doing it. I knew you could do this and that things would work out for you."

"I don't want to get my hopes up yet, but I have some shoots lined up and had other people reaching out, so I'm really excited and hopeful for it."

"I've never doubted you, Harper, and I know you can do this," Ava assured me. "It's almost like this whole ordeal was a blessing in disguise."

I mulled over her words for a moment. "You know what, maybe you're right."

Ava laughed. "I know I am."

We chatted until I was pulling back into my parking space at my apartment building. We ended our call with the promise of meeting up for lunch tomorrow. I tucked my phone back into my purse before heading to my apartment. The door was still locked when I had left it when I left earlier.

I slid the key in and turned the knob before slowly letting myself into the small space. It was quiet inside and I gently closed the door behind me. Nico must have still been in bed, which had me breathing a sigh of relief. I set my purse and keys down on the counter in the small kitchen area.

"Where were you, love?"

Chapter Thirty-one

Nico

I leaned against the doorframe to Harper's bedroom as I stared at her in the kitchen. My hands were lazily tucked in the front pockets of my sweats and I watched her carefully as she turned around to face me. A pink tint crept up her neck and spread across her cheeks as her eyes searched mine with a brief panic.

"I woke up and you were gone," I told her as I pushed away from the doorframe and began to close the distance between us.

Harper's slender throat bobbed and she nervously shifted her weight on her feet. "I went to have my meeting with Phillip."

My eyebrows pulled together as I stopped in front of her. "I thought it wasn't until tomorrow?"

"I spoke to him yesterday afternoon and we changed it to today."

I stared at her for a moment. "And you didn't want me to go along."

She shook her head at me. "It was something I needed to handle by myself."

"What happened to us figuring it out together?"

Harper stepped into my space and laced her hands together behind my neck. "I don't need you to fight all my battles for me, Nico. I love you but I also like my independence, and it's important to me that it's something I don't lose."

Her words hit me harder than I expected. I stared down at her as I slid my hands around her waist. "I would never ask you to give up your independence, love. If I'm ever overstepping, please just let me know. I promise that you won't hurt my feelings."

Her eyes widened as they searched mine. "So you're not mad at me?"

I lifted an eyebrow at her. "Why would I be mad at you? Do I wish you would have told me you changed the meeting? Absolutely, but there's no reason for me to be mad at you."

"Thank you," she said softly as a smile touched her lips. "I'm sorry I didn't tell you. I didn't want you to get mad that I changed it and I didn't want you to argue with me about coming along."

Laughter rumbled in my chest and I slid my hands down to cup the backs of her thighs as I lifted her up into the air. I gently set her down on the counter and stood between her legs. "I might be stubborn and I might argue, but if you tell me no to something I will always listen to you, Harper."

"You are pretty stubborn," she mused as she played

with the hair at the nape of my neck. "And you do like to argue."

"I never once told you anything differently. That's who I am, love. And where you're concerned, I will always be protective and overly opinionated."

She stared up at me as she hooked her legs around my lower back, pulling me flush against her. "You're so unapologetically you and I love it."

My face dipped down to hers. "Yeah, well, I love you."

"Not as much as I love you," she argued back with a smirk pulling on her lips.

"I beg to differ," I chuckled before claiming her mouth with mine. I breathed her in, my tongue sliding along the seam of her lips. She parted them and let me in as our tongues tangled together. She was the only thing that mattered to me and I would spend the rest of my life showing her that. No matter what came our way, we would always find a way to make it work.

Abruptly, I pulled away from her. "Does this mean you're going to move in with me now?"

Harper laughed and shook her head. "Nope."

"Dammit," I muttered, fighting the playful smirk that pulled on the corners of my lips. "What are your plans then?"

"I'm going to do my own thing," she said quietly but her tone was filled with confidence. "'I'm officially starting my own photography business to do what I love. I have enough money saved up and I think I have enough clients to get things started. All I can do is try to build from here and hope it turns into a real career."

I'd never felt more proud in my entire fucking life. Even the day I was drafted into the NHL didn't compare to watching Harper blossom and grow.

"I'm so fucking proud of you, love. You are so fucking amazing and I know you will go far with this."

She tilted her head to the side. "How can you be so sure?"

"Because I believe in you, Harper."

She fell silent for a moment as she stared back at me. "How would you feel about maybe staying here with me more often? You know… since Giana is going to be staying at your place."

My lips twitched. "Is this your way of asking me to move in with you without coming out and actually saying it?"

She shrugged and smiled shyly. "I don't want to ask you to give up your place or anything. I was just thinking that if you were here, we would be able to spend more time together and not have to go back and forth."

"Only if I can bring Ballsy with me."

Her eyes widened as she lifted her eyebrows. "You're kidding."

I shook my head. "You're not my only good luck charm. I need both of you in order to succeed."

"I don't know where we would put it. Can't you just go back to your place to see it when you need to?"

I laughed out loud and shook my head. "You don't understand how it works, do you?"

Harper stared at me. "You do whatever you need to do. If it needs to be here with you, then bring it along. I just thought if we stayed here, then your sister could have your place to herself."

"You mean, so then I can fuck you on every surface of your apartment without someone walking in on us?"

She half choked, half laughed. "You're bold."

"I just know what I want, love," I said matter-of-factly as my face dipped back down to hers. "And that's you."

Epilogue

Nico

One year later

As I walked out to the parking lot, I found Harper waiting for me by the VIP entrance. Since she didn't work for the team as their photographer anymore, she was able to come along to my games with me and watch them from the stands. It was a pretty amazing feeling when I scanned the crowds for her.

There was just something about having her here to watch rather than working her own job that made it have a different feel. It was like a special moment I was able to share with her, even if she wasn't able to be at the team level anymore like she used to be.

Harper's smile was bright when she spotted me and I couldn't fight the grin that took over my lips as I walked up to her. I wrapped my arms around her waist with my lips instantly finding hers. Harper kissed me back and I breathed her in, feeling her soft lips against mine.

"You looked amazing tonight," she said softly as I pulled away from her.

I wrapped my arm around the tops of her shoulders and pulled her flush against my side. "Not as amazing as you look every night."

"You know you don't have to try and charm me anymore," she laughed quietly as we headed out into the parking lot through the VIP entrance. The air was warm outside and I removed my arm from Harper so she could take off her coat. I instantly smiled as I saw her with my jersey on.

It was what she normally wore when she came to my games, but fuck me. Seeing her with my name and number on her back did something to me. Something deep down inside that made me want to lock her away and never let anyone have access to her but me.

"I'm not trying to charm you, love. Just stating the obvious." I grinned and winked as we reached my car. She pressed her back against the side of the car as I went to open the door, but I instantly abandoned it. Instead, I closed the space between us, entering her personal space within a fraction of a second.

I slid my hand along the side of her neck, cupping the back of her head before crashing my lips against hers. They were perfect and so fucking soft. She tasted like candy, and I wanted to live in this moment forever. Our bodies were flush against one another's and I pressed her against the side of the car as I kissed her breathless.

I wanted the oxygen in her lungs. I wanted the blood in her veins.

I. Wanted. All. Of. Her.

"Fuck," I murmured against her lips as I slowed our kiss. "There's something about seeing you wearing my jersey that drives me fucking crazy. I want to see you wearing nothing but my jersey."

Harper smirked against my mouth before nipping at my bottom lip. "How about I do one better and fuck you with it on instead?"

My tongue slid along the seam of her lips as I urged them open. Harper obeyed and I breathed her in once again. Our tongues tangled together in a rush and I couldn't get enough of her. I knew I needed to get her home, but I was ready to fuck her up against the side of my car instead. Fuck it all.

I pulled away, once again leaving both of us breathless. "I need you, Harper. I want you riding my cock with my number on your back."

Harper laughed softly and shook her head. "Not happening here," she said quietly. "We're standing in the middle of the parking lot, Nico."

I angled my chin down to look at her. "Well, I'm not waiting until we get home and I'm not fucking you in my car." I paused for a heartbeat before slowly taking a step back. I held my hand out to her. "Come with me."

"You better not be taking me to the locker room again," she said, her laughter floating around us as I led her back toward the building.

"Nope," I said with a grin as I looked down at her and led her inside. "You have to be quiet, though."

She pulled her lip in between her teeth and nodded. Everyone had already cleared out and I wasn't sure where the security guards were, but I didn't even care. Harper followed behind me until we were walking back through the locker room. She didn't question me as I led her down the tunnel toward the ice.

I stopped when we reached the door by the bench and glanced around, but there was no one to be seen anywhere. Quietly opening it, I pulled Harper through with me and our feet slid across the ice as we began to shuffle across it. She attempted to stifle a giggle as we almost lost our balance and went down.

We made our way across the ice and I opened the next door, pulling Harper inside with me. I turned around to face her and she stared up at me with a curious look.

"Why'd you bring me to the penalty box?"

A smile touched my lips. "Do you remember the first game you photographed? It was the first time we saw each other since that night at the club."

"Of course, I remember it. You ended up getting into a fight and got a penalty for it."

I nodded and smiled as I backed up until the backs of my knees were hitting the bench. Releasing Harper, I reached for the waistband of my pants and shifted them down along with my boxers as I took a seat and pulled my cock out.

"I figured it was only fitting if we ended up in the penalty box together," I murmured as I reached for her.

Harper pushed her own pants down to her ankles and left my jersey on as she closed the distance between us. She lifted her legs and straddled me on the bench. My cock was positioned against her and she slowly slid down the length of it until I filled her to the brim.

A moan escaped her and my hands gripped her hips as she began to move up and down. Her bright blue eyes glimmered as she stared down at me with a mischief dancing across her face.

"I will gladly meet you in the penalty box any day."

Extended Epilogue

Nico

The hot sun beat down on my back as I lay on my stomach next to Harper. Her eyes were closed and her hair was pulled up in a messy bun on top of her head. My eyes traveled across her sun-kissed skin, trailing over the strings of her bikini as I fought the urge to pull it off of her in front of everyone around us.

I lifted my head and surveyed the area. All of the other guests at the resort seemed preoccupied on the beach. Maybe no one would notice the two of us.

Rolling over, I sat up on the edge of my lounge chair as I stared at Harper. "Hey," I murmured as I reached over and slid my hand along her spine.

Harper lifted her hand to shield her eyes from the sun as she looked at me. A smile pulled on my lips as I watched the sunlight glimmer on the rock that was around her finger. *I did that. I made her my fucking wife.*

"What's wrong?" she questioned me with concern in her eyes as they bounced back and forth between mine. "Is everything okay?"

I nodded as I rose to my feet and held out my hand for her. "Everything is perfect. Come with me."

She raised an eyebrow at me but didn't question me as she got up from her lounge chair and slid her hand into mine. Her palm was warm against mine and I laced my fingers through hers as I led her closer to the water. The soft waves lapped at our feet as we stood ankle deep in the warm ocean.

Harper was silent as she stood next to me and we stared out at the water. We only had three days left here in paradise and then we would have to head back to reality. We waited until after the season was over to get married. That way we were able to have our honeymoon without worrying about any interruptions. It wasn't often that we had a lot of time together without other things going on.

I looked down at my beautiful wife and a smirk played on my lips as she looked up at me. Her bright blue eyes shone under the sunlight. I spun her around with me and we walked farther down the beach, away from where most of the other guests were.

There was a row of cabanas and they were all vacant as we moved closer to them. I glanced back at Harper and mischief danced in her eyes as her feet moved through the sand. I led her to the very last one, the one that was the farthest from everyone, and I pulled her down onto it with me.

She rolled onto her back as I leaned up on my knees and pulled the curtains shut. "What are you shutting those for?"

I turned back to her and slid my fingers under the

strings of her bikini. "Because no one needs to see what I'm about to do to you."

"You know those curtains won't block out the sound, right?" she questioned me as she lifted her hips into the air for me to remove her bikini bottoms.

Discarding them to the side, I pulled out my cock that was already fucking throbbing and settled in between her legs. She was wet as I settled in between her thighs and slid inside her in one fluid movement. She inhaled sharply, her manicured nails digging into my back as I filled her completely with one thrust.

"Then I guess you're just going to have to be quiet," I murmured as I nipped at her bottom lip. "You think you can be quiet while I fuck you senseless, love?"

Harper wrapped her legs around my waist as she hooked her feet behind my back and nodded. She stared up at me with those fucking ocean eyes of hers and I was so close to losing myself already.

"Good girl," I growled as my mouth collided with hers. I stole the air from her lungs and swallowed every moan that escaped her as I started to move my hips. Harper held on and I pounded her into the mattress of the cabana.

There was no way anyone on the outside wouldn't have some speculation as to what was going on behind the curtains with the way the entire thing was rocking. I didn't give a fuck. The only thing that mattered was Harper, and I was going to fuck my wife like she deserved to be fucked.

She took every thrust as I pounded into her with an urgency. As much as I wanted to take my time with her, this was a bit of a different situation. I didn't really want either of us to get caught, considering the fact that it was the middle of the day and there were people out everywhere. I wanted to be able to fuck my wife when I pleased, wherever and however I wanted.

I didn't need someone coming to interrupt us and telling us we couldn't do this here. So, instead we were going to have to settle for a quickie before I could get her back to our room where I could do what I wanted.

It wasn't long before Harper's legs tightened around my waist and she was shattering around me. Her pussy clenched around my cock as she drove me over the edge. I lost myself inside of her and we were both falling into an abyss of ecstasy.

"Holy fuck," I breathed as I rested my forehead against hers. We were both breathless as we came up for air. "I could stay like this forever."

Harper chuckled softly. "I don't think you could really play hockey if you were inside me."

"Don't tempt me, love. I could figure out a way to play with my cock balls deep inside this sweet pussy."

"You're ridiculous," she laughed and shook her head as I slowly pulled out of her.

I smiled down at her, my eyes traveling from my cum dripping from her pussy then back to her hooded gaze. "Yeah, but you love me."

"I do love you," she smiled back at me.

"Not as much as I love you," I retorted as I slid her feet back through the holes of her bikini bottoms.

Her eyebrows pulled together. "Why does everything always have to be a competition with you?"

I shrugged. "You did marry a hockey player. Did you expect something different?"

She shook her head as she pulled me back down to her. "Nope. I wouldn't want you any other way."

"Good," I murmured as my face dipped back down to hers. "Because you're stuck with me for an eternity."

Harper smiled her smile that was only ever reserved for me. "Promise?"

"I promise you," I said before capturing her mouth with mine as I sealed my promise with a kiss. Harper was the most unexpected thing to ever happen in my life but I never wanted to be without her.

And I would spend the rest of my life dedicating everything to this woman.

My woman.

My wife.

A LOOK INSIDE THE NEXT BOOK

The Tides Between Us is the second book in the Orchid City Series. It is a friends to lovers, disability rep romance that features Giana Cirone and a hot surfer who saves a turtle on the beach one day.

Continue reading for a look inside The Tides Between Us.

CHAPTER ONE
DECLAN

The lower half of my legs were submerged in the ocean as I floated in the water, just past the coastline where the waves break. It wasn't a good morning for surfing and the East Coast was nothing like the West when it came to their swells. The ocean gods weren't paying me any favors this morning, but I technically wasn't supposed to be surfing anyway.

At least the sunrise didn't disappoint.

I turned myself around on my board and watched the sky as it began to shift through a series of hues of color. The pinks transformed into yellow and orange, mixing together as the sun began to crest the horizon. It was quiet and peaceful. The ocean had a way of calming my soul.

Sunrise was always my favorite part of the day. The rest of the world was still waking up, but out here, the ocean was always full of life. Dolphin fins bobbed above the surface and a few jumped into the air. The sun poked up above the horizon and it cast its light across the ripples, creating a shimmering essence across the water. My eyelids fluttered shut and I inhaled deeply, filling my lungs with the salt-tinged air.

This was where I belonged.

I stayed out on the water until the sky had shifted into a bright blue, showcasing the sun. there wasn't a single cloud in sight. Rolling onto my stomach, I used my good arm to paddle until I met the waves and let them push me closer to the shore. Submerging both of my arms into the ocean, I gave one forceful push, feeling the twinge of pain in my left shoulder before I was able to hop off my board and carry it in.

A dislocated shoulder wasn't a death sentence. It wouldn't take surfing away from me, but it was undoubtedly an inconvenience. A month ago, I was at the Oahu Pro Classic in Hawaii. The water was choppy as hell as a storm was rolling in. I lost my balance while tube riding. The barreling wave was absolute perfection, but I slipped and tumbled into the water. My shoulder was pulled from its socket as the ocean tossed me around a bit.

It hurt like a bitch, but nothing compared to the feeling when the doctor popped it back in place. When I got back to Malibu, they told me my recovery would be three to four months. It wasn't ideal, but it wasn't the end of the world. I took the next flight out to Florida to bunker down with my brother in Orchid City. The waves were shit here and it wouldn't be as tempting and dangerous if I decided to hop on my board earlier than I was supposed to. The physical therapist I had been working with here was hopeful I would be looking at closer to twelve weeks rather than the full sixteen.

My feet sank into the sand as I walked to the shore. The granules scratched at my skin and I welcomed the feeling. I walked a few feet away from where the water met the beach and I turned once more to look back at the ocean. It was killing me to not be out there like I was used to, but I knew I had to be patient. I could not afford to fuck this up.

Something dark and peculiar caught my eye. At first glance, it looked like a horseshoe crab that had washed up, but the shape was different and it wasn't black. I propped my board up in the sand and began to walk over to investigate. My eyebrows pulled together and I squinted my eyes to get a better look as I closed the distance between myself and the object. There were streaks of bright red washing into the water.

As I got closer, I realized what I was looking at. I noticed the muddy-colored shell immediately, followed by the block-shaped head of the turtle. I didn't know much about turtles, but this one's shell was only about a foot and a half in circumference. Based on the way it looked, I figured it was a loggerhead, which was particularly common in this area. Growing up by the ocean, you quickly learned about the environment and the habitants of it.

My eyes traveled from the streaks of blood to the turtle as I began to scan it from a bit of a distance. It stared up at me with fright, but the pain was evident. It didn't even attempt to move away from me as it stayed exactly where it had washed up. As my gaze reached its front legs, I noticed there was fishing wire wrapped tightly around it, cutting through its flesh.

The damned thing was injured and it needed help.

Typically, you were supposed to call a hotline for someone to come pick the animal up, but as I watched the blood mix with the salty ocean water, I knew I couldn't just wait here with the turtle in hopes that someone would eventually arrive. A sigh escaped me and I shook my head momentarily before sliding my hands beneath the turtle and lifting it into the air.

It was almost as if the thing was paralyzed by fear, or perhaps the pain. Whatever it was, it didn't fight against me or try to escape. There was a facility less than a mile away. I just needed to get the turtle into the back of my Jeep and get it there.

"It's okay, dude," I told the turtle, like it had any understanding of English. My feet kicked up sand as I lengthened my strides while walking toward the road. "I'm gonna get you some help."

It was a short walk to the car and my shoulder was throbbing by the time I reached it. I laid down a towel and loaded the turtle into the trunk like it was completely normal. We stared at one another for a few moments before I shook my head to myself. What the hell was I doing?

I quickly sprinted back to the beach to grab my board and ran back to the Jeep. The turtle was in the same spot I left it and I strapped my surfboard to the roof before hopping in behind the wheel. Dust kicked up from the tires as I shifted into first gear and let off the clutch while pulling onto the road. I was careful while driving for the turtle's sake, but I needed to get it to the rehabilitation facility as quickly as I could.

It was less than a three-minute drive. The sign was just along the road. *Orchid City Marine Research & Rehabilitation Center.* I pulled my car down the long winding drive that led to the main building. There were four smaller buildings that I could see, scattered behind the main entrance. I stopped directly out front, not bothering to park in a parking spot.

I threw the vehicle in park, killed the engine, and hopped out before rushing around to the back of the Jeep. Part of the towel underneath the turtle's flipper was saturated with blood, but it appeared to have slowed down a bit. Using the towel to cradle the turtle, I lifted it into the air and removed it from my trunk. My movements were hesitant as I carried it to the front door, careful to not jar it at all.

The glass doors slid open as I stepped in front of them and a rush of cold air wrapped itself around me. It was quiet inside and my flip-flops were loud, echoing throughout the space as they slapped the linoleum floor. There was a woman with her back turned to me, but she didn't turn around as I walked up to the front desk area. I set the turtle down on the floor by my feet and stared at the back of her head.

Her long midnight hair was pulled back in a ponytail and she was filling up some syringes with liquid. I shifted my weight on my feet, my eyes scanning the curves of her body before landing on the back of her head once again.

"Excuse me," I said after a few more moments of

silence passed. She didn't turn to face me and I was growing impatient. The damn turtle was still bleeding and this woman was acting like I wasn't even here. She turned her head slightly, but still didn't acknowledge me. I watched her jaw as she was chewing something and I saw the opened strawberry Pop-Tart wrapper beside her. "Hello?" I said louder this time.

She was arranging the syringes in a tray and my eyebrows were pulled together as I gave the back of her head a perplexed look. I was extremely confused why she was ignoring me. A sigh escaped me and I moved around to the side of the desk until I was about to step behind it. She must have caught sight of me from the corner of her eye. She whipped her head to the side, her lips parting slightly as her bright blue eyes widened.

Holy shit. My breath caught in my throat and I was instantly captivated by her. Her features were completely symmetrical and my eyes traveled across the planes of her face. Her cheekbones were high and prominent, her nose perfectly straight. For a moment, I forgot what I was even doing here.

She smiled brightly at me and her eyes were warm and welcoming. I couldn't fucking breathe.

"I brought a turtle," I said in a rush as I ran an anxious hand through my tousled waves. My hair was still damp from the ocean and I pushed the locks away from my face. I instantly wanted to take the words back as I realized how stupid they sounded. "I found an injured turtle on the beach and I brought it in."

She moved her hands, twisting them around with her arms as she moved her fingers. Her lips moved simultaneously; however, she remained silent. The dots connected and it clicked in my brain. She wasn't ignoring me. She didn't even know I was there talking to her because she couldn't hear me.

I tilted my head to the side as I tried to read her lips, but quickly realized how terrible I was at it. Realization struck her and her face faltered slightly. She shook her head apologetically and picked up a notepad beside her. Her hand moved quickly as she wrote on the paper.

Where is the turtle? How badly is it injured?

I looked at the paper and went to reach for it to write back to her. Her bright blue eyes met mine as she shook her head again and wrote something else down.

I can read lips.

I nodded. "It's over here," I motioned to the side of me. "There's wire wrapped around its flipper and it was bleeding on the beach. I know we're supposed to call stuff like this in, but I couldn't just leave it on the beach to potentially bleed out."

She followed me around to the front of the desk area and she crouched down as she inspected the turtle. Silence settled between us, although there was some sense of comfort in it. She held her finger up to me before she scooped the turtle up and rushed through one of the doors behind the desk.

Curiosity got the better of me. I followed after her, stepping back into the hospital area of the facility. She was a few strides ahead of me and I watched her as she ducked into another room. I stopped just inside the doorway as she set the turtle down on a metal table. Two people in scrubs were instantly looking at it, signing questions to her, and she signed back to answer.

The one guy who was looking at the turtle's flipper caught sight of me and lifted his gaze to mine. He nodded his head and the woman spun on her heel to face me. I watched as she signed something to the other staff members once more before marching toward me. Her palm was soft and her hand was small as she wrapped it around my wrist. She walked past me, turning me around with her as she led me back toward the lobby.

I couldn't fight the smile that pulled on my lips.

She didn't stop until we reached the front desk and she was grabbing for the notepad and pen again.

You can't be back there. It's for staff only.

I shrugged with indifference. "What about the turtle? Will you guys be able to help it?"

She nodded before scribbling another note on the piece of paper. *We won't know for sure, but it definitely could have been worse. That turtle is lucky you found her when you did.*

"Pop-Tart," I said abruptly, which had her giving me a quizzical look. "Her name is Pop-Tart."

You named her?

I shrugged again. "It felt like she needed a name instead of just referring to her as 'that turtle'. Don't you guys name the animals anyways?"

She smiled brightly and nodded.

We do. Pop-Tart sounds like the perfect name for her.

"When will you know more about what will happen with her?"

I watched her delicate hand as she began to write something again. I was officially invested in this turtle's recovery and I wanted an excuse to see her again.

Check back in a few days. We should have more concrete information then.

"Perfect, I'll check back in then." I smiled back at her. "I didn't get your name."

She raised an eyebrow and wrote it down.

Giana.

"Declan." I held my hand out to her. "Have a good rest of your day, Giana."

My eyes lingered on her face a moment longer and the silence settled between us as she offered me a smile and a nod. I loved the way her name felt rolling off my tongue. I left her without another word, except the promise that was left hanging in the silence.

I was a patient man.

I could wait a few days before seeing Giana again.

ABOUT THE AUTHOR

Cali Melle is a contemporary romance author who loves writing stories that will pull at your heartstrings. You can always expect her stories to come fully equipped with heartthrobs and a happy ending, along with some steamy scenes and some sports action. In her free time, Cali can usually be found spending time with her family or with her nose in a book. As a hockey and figure skating mom, you can probably find her freezing at a rink while watching her kids chase their dreams.

ALSO BY CALI MELLE

WYNCOTE WOLVES SERIES

Cross Checked Hearts

Deflected Hearts

Playing Offsides

The Faceoff

The Goalie Who Stole Christmas

Splintered Ice

Coast to Coast

Off-Ice Collision

ORCHID CITY SERIES

Meet Me in the Penalty Box

The Tides Between Us

Written In Ice

STANDALONES

The Lie of Us

Made in the USA
Las Vegas, NV
05 January 2024

83841511R00194